GIFTS OF THE FOREST

BY

LINDA STUTRUD SCHEET

Gifts of the Forest

ISBN: 978-0-9845917-1-8

Cover Design by Phil Davis, Flip Design Studio

Interior Design by Amanda Heinrich, AGraphicStyle

Published by Spiritus Communications, Inc.

DEDICATION

This book is dedicated
to my three children who, through all our chaos,
still have a degree of connectedness;
to Ken, who kept encouraging me to write; and
to Stara, who brought me back to my love of horses.

CHAPTER 1

In Minnesota, school started the Tuesday after Labor Day weekend. This particular fall's weather was affected by spring's late start. Summer extended itself into fall, making the school days summer-hot.

Not knowing how to dress for the weather, most of the staff and students wore summer clothing, supplemented with a sweater for comfort in the building. When confronting the initial burst of hot air upon leaving the air-conditioned building in late afternoon, the sweater was cast aside.

Out of the learning center student body, at least one student inevitably would show up wearing noticeably short shorts. The center's teachers would send the scantily dressed student to see the school social worker, Sarah Westgard, to check out the apparel. If needed, Sarah had a discussion with the student about the school dress policy. Usually Sarah gave the mostly-female students the opportunity to change their clothing—either into something they had with them or something their parents later brought to the school. But the third option was to change into another pair of shorts or T-shirt supplied by the school. The pair of long jogging shorts kept on-hand, however, normally did not meet the student's approval. If no resolution could be reached, the student was sent home.

Playing police to the dress code was not one of Sarah's favorite duties. As the harbinger of humility and modesty, the discussion seldom went well. Students did not buy the "distraction of the education process" theory. They generally left the office with the inclination that Sarah was a prude or meddling. Over time, the relationship between Sarah and the student may develop into a more positive one, but this interaction definitely did not create an amicable start.

It was, however, important to Sarah that she ultimately could develop a trusted relationship with her students. She hoped they could learn that she was fair. But these interactions left her feeling concerned that she would need to make up lost ground.

Here we go again, Sarah thought, watching Jazabel enter her office. Jazabel was a new student, the first to shadow Sarah's doorway this term. Approximately 5 feet, 8 inches, the 14-year-old looked like a volleyball player with her long, tan legs. Her light brown hair shone as it reached her mid back, and her make-up was perfect: not too much, not too little. *She obviously took her time getting ready for school,* Sarah thought. *I doubt this will go well.*

Jazabel had been referred from the eighth grade to the area learning, which was a part of the public-school district sometimes known for having the "troublemakers." The center fought this identity. They had a smaller student population with more resources for tracking the students' attendance and achievement, and the staff aimed to make a difference in students' lives.

Jazabel had shown a lack of attendance and productivity at the regular school setting, thus needing a tailored ninth-grade program that the area learning center could provide. Studies had shown that failure to thrive in the ninth grade was an indicator for high school dropout. The hope was that Jazabel could be put on track for graduation. She was not happy about the referral to the center; it meant she would not attend school at the high school campus. But her dad insisted she give it a try.

Jazabel walked into the office quietly, sat down, and gave no information unless asked, at which time she politely rationed answers. Jazabel looked around the office. There was a laminated poster of Maya Angelou hanging on Sarah's wall and a rainbow triangle magnet on the beige file cabinet—but not much more to prepare Jazabel for who this social worker was. Jazabel's shorts were short, but something else caught Sarah's eyes. Jazabel had a tattoo that peeked out of her T-shirt neckline, and maybe all the way down her body, as it also appeared out of her shorts on her inner thigh. It looked freshly made, by the appearance of raised, pinkish skin at its base.

And it looked sore. Sarah thought about Jazabel's well-being. *Of course, she would not want to wear clothing that would rub on it, so maybe that is why she is bearing so much skin.* Her T-shirt looked soft and loose; pants would rub.

The tattoo grabbed Sarah's attention again. It was simple and black, rather large, and appeared to be an inscription of some kind.

"Is that a new tattoo?" asked Sarah.

Jazabel shifted in her chair, looking down at the part of her tattoo that appeared on her thigh and smiling as if proud of it. "It is, just healing," replied Jazabel, thinking, *stupid question, anyone could tell it's fresh.*

Sarah pondered the alternate idea that Jazabel was wearing her short shorts to show off the tattoo.

"It looks a little sore. Have you applied anything to diminish the tenderness?" asked Sarah.

Jazabel fumed silently. First, she had been called into Sarah's office about her clothing, and now this stranger was in her business. *The bitch* was asking personal questions. *Diminish the tenderness, what the hell! Does she think I am an idiot? Like she even knows how a tattoo feels, or what it means.*

Jazabel was livid that Sarah, someone with no clue what was appropriate for a student to wear to school or for any occasion, was advising her as if they were friends. To Jazabel, Sarah appeared to be wearing her "old hippie lady who forgot to change her style for the last four decades" clothing. *Sarah, the hippie lady*, Jazabel thought as she smiled to herself.

Sarah would have agreed with the assessment of having no style. Being a middle child meant hand-me-downs and no attention paid to what was currently in fashion. She simply wore comfortable clothing.

Sarah also never knew when she would need to be on the move at school, thus heels and dresses may not be an asset. Additionally, Sarah carried the scars of her past relationships, including a mentally ill sibling who had criticized everything in her surroundings. Since the sibling had shared a bedroom with Sarah, that usually meant Sarah was the closest target for attacks—for dressing, singing or even breathing.

Then there was the ex-husband's verbal abuse, which gave her no reason to think she could wear clothing with style.

Away from her sibling and ex-husband, she still justified her lack of "current" clothing. She thought she had better things to put her money into besides her wardrobe. Her motto was: *if you don't buy it, there is money in your pocket*. Sarah had provided for three children, so her wardrobe seemed a low priority.

As for the tattoos, she was just too cheap to get a tattoo.

Jazabel sensed there might be trouble brewing. This nosy lady was acting as if she cared about her tattoo, but she knew that Sarah had been asking too many questions for reasons other than her *thigh was sore* or *shorts were too short*. Sarah was a social worker, who Jazabel considered to be *nothing but snitches*.

Jazabel's family consisted of her father and brother. While her father was a drunk, her mother was a druggy. At this point in Jazabel's life, the family had no idea where Mom was—possibly on the streets of a larger city or hanging with a new local pimp.

When Jazabel was little, her father had been drinking and left Jazabel alone for the night. The next morning, her brother stayed home, taking advantage of the opportunity. Jazabel enjoyed learning. When she did show up, she came to school unkempt and still wearing her pajamas.

As a child, Jazabel had craved the attention her mostly female teachers gave her when she worked hard. She did not have to try too hard, since learning came easy for her.

But even back then, Jazabel's wardrobe became an issue. The elementary school social worker had believed showing up for school in pajamas was reportable. Since she could not send an early elementary age child home without adult supervision, she "snitched" on her and called the county.

The only outcome from the incident was Jazabel was taken from the home for a few weeks and placed with a "fake" family for the duration. Feeling like a stranger while eating food that was alien to her pallet and sleeping in an unfamiliar room made the two weeks seem like forever.

When she was returned home by the county, she caught both verbal and physical abuse, which were all too familiar. Jazabel felt she had been responsible for any distress her family went through.

Jazabel learned to keep her mouth shut and not trust social workers. In this moment, she would not even display her distaste for the person sitting across from her. That may give too much of herself away.

Sarah, on the other hand, was genuinely concerned for Jazabel's well-being after seeing the tattoo. *Where does the tattoo meet under her shorts and T-shirt? Does it travel across the whole front her body?* she wondered. Jazabel was only 14. *A tattoo salon would not have administered the procedure without parental permission.*

"Where did you get the tattoo?" Sarah asked, trying to sound nonchalant.

Beautiful, young Jazabel with that long, golden-brown hair knew exactly what Sarah was getting at with her question. She sat smugly and said, "I know someone who had a tattoo gun, and he did it for me."

Sarah listened closely to Jazabel, hoping she would say a little too much. As she sat, she thought about how beautiful her female student's hair was. *The Native American girls with long, fine, black hair; Hispanic girls with long, slightly curly, brown locks; African American with their free style; and White girls with their shiny hair enchanted by natural highlights.* Sarah considered the beauty of the diverse clients she served. When the Muslim girls gave Sarah the privilege of seeing their hair, it seemed to be so healthy and full. She saw an occasional blue head of hair, adding a creativity to the realm of styles. Sarah sat with her short, fine, Norwegian hair, which never really grew much, and felt no comparison to her students' fine locks.

Jazabel smoothed her hair into a ponytail, wound it around, and put it on top of her head, then wrapped it around itself in a quick motion, using a hair tie to create a messy but cute bun on her head.

Back to task, thought Sarah. During her visit to the office, Jazabel had offered limited information—no name of the tattoo artist nor meaning of the symbolism. In fact, Jazabel became increasingly defensive about her shorts while becoming more secretive about how a tattoo got on her neckline and inner thigh. Jazabel knew she needed to mask her irritation concerning this office visit as much as she could, so as not to draw attention to the situation. It was difficult, but Jazabel did not want Sarah to know how she felt.

Sarah sensed Jazabel's irritation through her cool politeness. She was aware of issues beyond Jazabel's wardrobe: She had been couch-hopping. Her father had called the school several times that day wondering if his daughter had made it to the first day of school. Knowing his daughter was in school was the only way her dad could know that Jazabel was safe.

After not getting any answers about the tattoo or an agreement to change her clothing, Sarah let Jazabel know she was calling her parents about her clothing. There was no contact information for Jazabel's mother in the school directory. The story was her mother had simply left the family and lived with her druggie boyfriend, which was already known by Sarah. In the student information, "data for mother" appeared as: contact information unknown. Her dad, Ralph, had begun recovery and was getting strong enough to set ground rules for his daughter. Jazabel was confused by these new rules and wondered where her father had been when she was younger and needed them. *Where was he when her mother needed a sober, caring person in her life?*

As Sarah called Ralph, Jazabel commented, "He is not

at home and probably won't answer anyway." Sarah had heard that before from students. Another good one was, "My parents don't like you; they won't answer the phone." All this young female had known until the "magical recovery" was verbal abuse from her father and physical abuse from her brother. In her mind, there was simply no help or parenting from Dad. *Too little too late*, thought Jazabel, as she considered herself an adult at 14.

Ralph answered. Sarah asked him to come to the school. He could either get his daughter and take her home because of the shorts or bring in a change of clothing.

Sarah was hoping her father would come in. She planned to use this interaction to mention the tattoo during their conversation. The shorts were very short, and the tattoo disappeared under them until it appeared again at the T-shirt neckline. The tattoo was more disturbing to Sarah than anything in that moment.

As it was, Ralph was fully aware of the tattoo and was going to turn the freak who violated his daughter's body into the law. Ralph felt guilty for all that his daughter had gone through. He also felt responsible for her choices. *And no, his daughter was not going home; it was too hard to get her to school.*

It seemed difficult to understand, but Ralph had given Jazabel permission to stay with a friend if she agreed to attend school. They fought so much, Ralph wanted to negotiate school attendance so the court would stay off their backs and home would not be a constant war zone. In Ralph's eyes, the current problem was her friend's influences on his daughter. But at least this decision was a start for healing their relationship—a process that would take time, one day at a time.

Jazabel and her friend stayed where they wanted, which made transportation to school difficult. But for the family's harmony, the arrangement had been made.

Ralph brought a soft pair of jogging pants for Jazabel to wear, a peace offering to show he had considered her comfort. As he walked into the office, Sarah observed how Jazabel and Ralph looked alike. He had light brown hair and the same "don't give me shit" twinkle in his eyes as his daughter. She agreed to wear the pants.

Dad felt guilt for the tattoo and for all his missed steps in parenting that led his daughter to her circumstances. A sadness dominated the anger in his voice, as he talked about his beautiful daughter and the tattoo.

While Ralph handed Jazabel the garment, he quietly inquired, "Will I see you after my shift is over?"

"Maybe." Jazabel flashed a smile back that was filled with complicated emotions—manipulation of her father's love and knowledge that she had just lied to him. *That is not happening*, thought Sarah.

For the moment, the crisis of the shorts was over, but the tattoo issue was not.

CHAPTER 2

It was an intense day. After the interaction with Jazabel, Sarah encountered one problem-solving event after another—from finding the address of an elementary student who was homeless so that he could be dropped off safely to determining the menu for the school's family night.

Sarah was grateful she had met Ben several summers ago. That summer, her friend had dragged her to a nearby, small-town, street dance. The evening was extremely humid, trapping the smell of keg beer with the country music in the air. The small town's Main Street was blocked by sawhorses creating a concrete dance floor, lined with local families and singles out to help celebrate their town's existence.

Sarah was dancing with the ladies when she decided she wanted to ask a man to dance. She knew enough not to ask a male who did not seem interested in the music. Generally, she had learned to assume that those men were not dancers and would awkwardly refuse her request.

She spotted a man drinking a beer and watching the dancers. He was cute, proportionally built, with curly, grey hair and light hazel, brown eyes. He was wearing a blue, buttoned shirt and shorts.

His big negative was he was wearing socks with sandals. One of Sarah's female students had said she always judged a guy by the shoes he was wearing. *Ben would not pass the shoe apparel test.* Sarah laughed at herself as she glanced down at his footwear and realized she was considering her student's criteria to choose a dance partner.

Her dance partner, Ben, feeling a need to explain his appearance, said, "I am a glider instructor." Later Sarah learned that Ben had been flying since he was 18. The gliders would get sauna-hot on a humid, summer's day. The buttoned, blue shirt and socks were worn to follow the dress code for the Civil Air Patrol. He had been gliding with the CAP as part of the town's celebration. Hence, there he stood with shorts, socks, and sandals.

Ben had been observing the ladies dance in time with the music. *Dancing with the beat seems more natural for women,* he thought. He had noticed Sarah; she was wearing a simple summer dress and was not overly made up, with her chin-length, fine, blonde hair. He thought she was *attractive but not drop-dead gorgeous.* He watched as she followed her friend around, thinking it seemingly not her thing to be there at the dance.

Ben was a trained ballroom dancer, just one of his many skills. He had been hoping to dance that night. He felt innate fear of rejection when he asked someone to dance, but Sarah made it easy by approaching him first. That night of a few dances on the street began their relationship.

With their children all grown up, they could focus on building their lives towards retirement. Sarah's children were Stara, who was 21 and at her first real job; Levi, who was 25; and Dylan, who was 30. Ben's son, Mathew, was 28, and his daughter, Isabel, was 33.

Over the years, Ben and Sarah danced, they gardened, they traveled—but Ben was also a workaholic. Work always came first.

Workaholic or not, Ben liked having a female in his life. He liked it so much he had been married three times. Work, flying airplanes, and farming came first. *Work hard, play hard* was his motto. Sarah did not really mind; her job was very consuming. But when she was with Ben, she wanted it to be *her* time—with no preoccupation with telephone calls or last-minute arrangements for the next project. Over the years, she learned it did not always turn out that way.

One of the nice bonuses of dating Ben was his farm in the country. Sarah headed to the farm to de-stress many times before her retirement.

CHAPTER 3

Several days after Sarah's first encounter with Jazabel, Sarah and the Hispanic/Native American school liaison worker, Karla, were given a home visit to complete. Karla was a valuable part of the team. Besides speaking Spanish and Ojibwe, which reflected her own biracial background, she had grown up in a White foster home. Even though she did not have a degree, she had a unique ability based on her own background to find families and get answers about what was going on in the home that affected the students' attendance.

This home visit assignment was to go out to a sixth-grade male student's home and assist him with attending school regularly. The student was staying with his dad; his mother was in Texas. The boy was not coming to school, so Sarah and Karla were assigned to check on what was affecting his attendance.

Coincidentally, it was the same house Jazabel was known to stay at occasionally. Sarah was unaware of the comings and goings of the household except that some students would couch hop at this address.

It was set up to be just a routine home visit for the two. Sarah knocked on the door, and a young lady in her early twenties answered. Upon introducing themselves as school staff, the student's stepmother said that her husband, Michael, was upstairs. A little toddler with curly hair hung around her legs. *How absolutely adorable*, Sarah thought.

"Michael! Come down here and meet these ladies from the school who are here to see you," the stepmom shouted, seating herself on the steps in the corridor to watch the scene unfold. Another woman entered the front corridor, looking much like the stepmother.

"This is my sister," the stepmother said, offering no names in her introduction. The sister was followed by her toddler who looked almost like a twin to the one Sarah had admired.

While the young wife sat on the steps, she crossed her legs, raising her dress to reveal her inner leg. *She has the same tattoo as Jazabel*, Sarah noticed. Looking at the two young ladies, the two young toddlers, and then up at the steps, Sarah watched as a middle-aged, chubby man descended saying, "I always like meeting ladies." The wife's sister raced out of the entrance after her son. Sarah saw the tattoo on the back of her neck. *One can see the tattoo on a woman coming or going*, Sarah thought, *especially if they are nude or scantily dressed.*

What is going on here? Sarah wondered. *Something isn't right.* She sickened at the thoughts looming in her head. But she tried to slow her thinking and focus on the conversation. She was trying to record every detail as it happened, while appearing to be casual.

Her mind jumped to the worst case. *Was this man tattooing, virtually branding, young women and possibly having babies with them? What else?* Sarah felt herself becoming ill at her thoughts.

Michael, seemingly unconcerned by two school workers showing up at his house, gregariously joined the group. He was full of information: His son had been sick. His son's friends were regular visitors at the home. Any food in the refrigerator was free for the teenagers to eat. Young people had come over with a cold, which they had passed on to his son. Michael did not have his own health insurance for his son, so getting his son into a clinic to verify why he had missed so many days of school for illness was difficult. Besides, he knew that a cold would not be seen as a good enough reason for such an extreme lack of attendance. He was slowly agreeing on the importance of school attendance.

"I let the kids come and go here," Michael explained, trying to distract from the attendance issue. "I want them to feel welcome, so we treat them all like family. They know they can get what they need, even if that's a place to crash. What's mine is theirs!" Sarah saw through Michael's charm and reported generosity. She determined that his operation was based on a distorted Maslow's Hierarchy of Needs. He provided the basic needs of the teenagers: shelter and food, and then drugs. In time, the teens felt they belonged there. Once they were comfortable, he exploited them.

This is not a good man, Sarah thought. *He is sick, even evil*. Sarah desperately wanted to leave, to flee him, but she was aware she needed to get more information.

Michael knew he was rambling but wanted to seem friendly and give enough information that the two ladies would not need to come back to his house. *Especially the white social worker*, he thought, *they are always meddling into people's business*.

He would try to connect with Karla, to get her to join the conversation and trust him. Thus, throughout the whole conversation, Michael focused his attention on Karla, who he decided was a *cute little Hispanic woman*. In his mind,

Sarah was a white social worker, majorly conservative and judgmental. How could she understand me and the rules I live by? She's middle class and probably works just to occupy her time.

Michael dismissed Sarah without knowing the pain she had endured. He did not know that Sarah had not had the easy, middle class life he had assumed. Middle class to Sarah included the continual struggle of working up the ladder of society. Sarah had started late. She had dropped out of college and married a hometown farmer's son, Hank. He worked hard but drank his worries away the best he could and took his stress out on Sarah verbally. After years of verbal abuse, he became his words to her: ugly and mean. She left him, taking their three children—Dylan, Levi, and Stara—and the wounds and scars with her. As beautiful as her children were, the family life was not, and she did not want them to witness any more abuse.

Sarah had needed to support her family, so when she uprooted her three children, she moved to a college town where she earned her social work degree. She often wondered if that had been the right decision. She knew she had been right to leave her husband and probably should have done it sooner. But not staying geographically closer to her family for support left her with guilt. Living near her children's grandparents would have been better for her children. In getting her degree, she had put herself into situations she would never have experienced if she had remained on the farm—which enriched her life. But she'd taken her children away from their family and support system. And with the stress of being a single parent, Sarah often was angry and tired—not the best mood for nurturing her children.

Sarah knew what she was looking at in Michael, but Michael did not know her. That was not his role, nor did she want him to understand her or even try. *In this situation*, she convinced herself, *my history is unimportant. What is important are the children.*

Michael's actions and conversation were continually directed toward Karla, subtly letting Sarah know that neither she nor her judgement were welcomed. She did not mind the rudeness, because it gave her a chance to watch the conversation unfold. She knew Michael was trying to schmooze Karla with words: "You know how it is... You really know what I'm thinking."

But Karla also knew his game. She knew when a child was taken care of or when a child was abused. And those teens were *children in his house, children being abused*.

However, Karla, a professional at navigating these stomach-turning incidents, didn't let contempt keep her from responding calmly: "Would you like us to start transportation tomorrow for your son?" Michael acted overly pleased to know that transportation would start. "Of course, that would be great! Set that up, and I'll have him on the bus tomorrow."

The whole situation was very sickening to Sarah, as she watched him dance around with those words, trying to groom everyone in the room. But Sarah and Karla were onto his game.

When the two returned to the van, Sarah turned to Karla and said, "Usually people reveal the good side of themselves, then eventually the bad side appears through stress or other events. Michael could not hide his true side. He was such a snake, everything he did or said seemed to have a purpose for his own pleasure or satisfaction."

Karla reinforced Sarah's feeling by saying, "I really need to get back to school and wash my hands to rid myself of him." It wasn't Karla's first time on this rodeo ride: a home visit where she learned way more than students' educational needs from the interaction. Karla's focus was always on the children's needs. She resented the system all the way, but whatever she could do to make it right for students, she did.

Sarah and Karla made a good team.

After getting settled in the school van, Karla fumbled with the buttons and volume on the two-way radio to let staff know to re-add the young male student's name to transportation. She could not easily focus on the simple task before her. The home visit had distressed her.

Arriving at the school, Sarah and Karla reported everything they had heard and seen to the school officer. He promptly called the station.

Later he called them back into his office. "Don't do another home visit at that house without a police escort," he said.

They nodded in agreement. That was a very interesting request to them, but nothing else was shared. The secrecy was not unusual. If there was an open investigation or surveillance going on, most of the work went on behind the scenes.

Sarah self-debriefed by getting to the farm before dark and harvesting as many tomatoes as possible. She transformed the bright red tomatoes into hot sauce. Simple, repetitive, traditional activities cleared Sarah's mind. When her children were still at home, she shifted from social worker to mother quickly, as practical tasks that created something tangible helped her de-stress.

The students' stories had a room in her mind. At times they gently knocked at the door to be let out.

Sarah knew Jazabel's story would want to be released again from the closed door, but not tonight. Tonight was salsa-making night.

CHAPTER 4

There were days when Jazabel came to school so disoriented and uncooperative, she could not find her schoolwork or remember her schedule. Then there were days when Jazabel would stop into Sarah's office and chat about the incidental things important to young teens.

Through these chats, Sarah learned Jazabel loved animals. Jazabel believed it was important to treat them kindly.

Secretively, Jazabel would stop in to get a handle on what Sarah might know or planning to do about Jazabel's situation. She wanted to make sure she was a step ahead of Sarah. She needed to be careful if she started asking questions, because Sarah would return with her own questions. *Sneaky lady.*

Accidentally, she started to like Sarah. Not that she totally trusted her, but she began to think the *outdated hippie lady was okay*. The irony of the hippy lady nickname was that Sarah never really liked that hippie stuff, at least in the traditional sense. She was more of a small-town, farm girl.

To Sarah's credit, she had earned some of that trust. Jazabel had believed she could trust only her best friend, Emma, but she had purposely told Sarah things about her family, and the information had not resurfaced.

Emma and Jazabel used together and slept around together. They watched each other's backs. When Jazabel was in the office, she shared very little about her life on the streets. She did not share with Sarah that her tattoo actually itched when she needed a high; and when she was feeling the urge to get high, she would do whatever it would take to get comfortable.

Whether stealing or sleeping with many different men, there had really been nothing Jazabel had said no to, but Emma was there to make sure she would be safe, they told themselves. Yet they overestimated their power to protect one another. "Safety" was different to them than to Sarah. If one of them passed out, the other protected her friend from predators looking for sexual favors. Nothing was verbalized in any formal agreement, but it was known those favors were given in exchange for drugs, food, and housing. Otherwise, they thought they were taking advantage of the predators—keeping them company while they got a free fix.

On Fridays, Sarah would host NA/AA meetings at school. She would announce the school breakfast openly, but would quietly give certain students invitations for the lunch meeting. Those invitations went to the students that Sarah knew were required in their probation contract to attend a weekly meeting—or the ones who she sensed could benefit from dipping their toes in sobriety. If those students only wanted to be sober and straight for that one lunch hour, Sarah would take it.

Every week, Sara's AA connection, who she had met through a recovery program, would bring in community speakers. Some of the speakers were young, and they really connected with the students. Sarah and her AA connection became appreciative of each other for their dedication to the youth. The speakers would have a weekly "home meeting," which is where they felt safest. If the area learning center students wanted a home meeting beyond the one at school, speakers would give out their cell phone numbers and offer rides. The school meeting also helped create a support system for any student who may have a family member that used and openly rejected sobriety.

The sponsors had the unique role of presenting sobriety as "fun." Occasionally a student found a sponsor, but it was still difficult for the center's students to sustain sobriety in their unhealthy environment.

Being high was so important to Jazabel, she sold her shoes and traded much more for the high. When Sarah quietly gave Jazabel an invitation to the lunch meeting, she told Sarah she would be at the meeting, then cut out of school right before it started.

Jazabel was beginning to respect Sarah. She had a hard time saying no. At the time of their interaction, she did intend to go to the meeting, but when the meeting time came, it was *not happening*.

Demonstrated by Jazabel's' attendance and behavior, it was apparent that Jazabel and a few other center students had a hard time with a full day of school. Their ability to get along with others and staff were symptoms of their greater need for developing empathy and respect for authority and peers. This deficit caused stress across the board, but more importantly, their constant consequences taught the students they were failures.

Jenna, the area learning center's director, asked Sarah to think about a "learn-and-serve" project that could be structured for the students who struggled to end a full day positively. Jenna would often challenge Sarah with theory, and Sarah would run with the ideas and make them practical.

In the process, Sarah developed an opportunity to take students out to an animal rescue ranch for a project. *Giving back to the community should build the students' self-confidence and hopefully assist in their development of empathy*, Sarah thought.

Ben did not like the idea of Sarah driving some of the hardest-to-handle students out of town alone. Even in the late winter, it was almost dark by the time she got back into the metro area, and Sarah still needed to drop off the students in the community. Despite his concern, he only showed concern and listened—as Sarah shared stories, confidentially, of course.

Why does she carry on about confidentiality? he wondered. *Like I would know them anyway.* It angered him to hear some of the stories. He knew how hard the staff worked at the center. The disrespect displayed by some of the students was difficult for him to understand.

But the problem was much more deeply rooted in the students and through their family and community experience than he realized. A simple adjustment to correct their disrespect did not exist. Time, relationship development, and connectedness was needed. If a simple correction were enough to repair the damage to their lives, it would be a welcomed answer.

When Jazabel was asked if she wanted to join the learn-and-serve group that would go to an off-site animal shelter and earn her school credit, she agreed immediately. Jazabel was smart and wanted to finish high school. Sadly, her behavior was not driving her toward that goal.

Sarah filled the van with referred students and some who Sarah handpicked. Sarah could use the driving time to build relationships with the students. *Hopefully*, she thought, *employment skills and interpersonal skills will develop while working at the site*. Additionally, the outing gave everyone a break from the full day of desk time in school.

The van ride took 25 minutes of mostly highway driving with a short, gravel road leading into the ranch. The passengers would talk and share music. Sometimes they would share things with each other, not realizing Sarah could hear everything. Sarah never gossiped about the information, but if it was mandated reportable, she needed to do that.

The rescue ranch had initially been a typical farm converted first into a horse ranch—with a more than adequate barn containing stables and a small, indoor round pen. Occasionally, the county would ask the owner to take in an animal. It quickly became apparent the county had a need for a rescue farm to take in larger, abused animals in great numbers. The owner applied for a non-profit license, and the rescue ranch grew exponentially. They took in goats, pigs, mini horses, horses, donkeys, and fowl. Every inch of green space was fenced with electric wire to accommodate their growth. The pasture around the barn was reserved for the high-need horses.

Jazabel seemed to understand their needs and found an isolated area to muck. She had no need to interact with the staff. She was a good worker. She cleaned stables and groomed the horses without a complaint—actually, without saying a word. She just attended to her duties as if the action were therapeutic. Her weekly dedication made a difference. It put a small nick in a boulder of need.

Some days, Jazabel would forget to dress appropriately for the task. Perhaps she was not where her mucking clothes were when she woke up. She may have worn white jeans to school, but that did not stop her. Jazabel was committed to doing what she needed to do so that the rescue animals could have a more comfortable life. It gave her a sense of purpose and carved out a safe place for both Jazabel and the animals. Jazabel created a world for the creatures that was as nurturing as possible, providing what no one in her life had given her.

Sarah watched the way that Jazabel interacted with the animals and felt relief in witnessing that she seemed to know what nurturing was. Sarah saw hope that Jazabel could find a way through her own trauma.

The world at the rescue ranch was as different from Jazabel's real world as the animal's previous world had been for them. The pigs, dogs, horses, goats, and fowl were being watered, fed, and kept warm in a caring environment. Not every animal there learned to trust; some were still dangerous to be around. Some rebelled as they broke out of their pens whenever possible. The need for the familiar, combined with the need to run, was an astronomically difficult behavior pattern to break.

Jazabel was young, but she knew what she needed to do to get what she wanted. And on this particular day, what she wanted was not to sit in a van with Sarah or be delivered to the door of her home before she was ready to adhere to her father's rules. She wanted freedom and partying.

Jazabel had been a star worker all day. Sarah had no idea what Jazabel had planned.

Jazabel stepped out of the van when Sarah dropped off another student. "I need to get my jacket liner from Anne," explained Jazabel.

"Okay, hurry up. We are running late," requested Sarah.

Jazabel did need her jacket liner; that was true. But while out of the van, Jazabel took the opportunity to run away, becoming the first student Sarah had lost on a field trip.

The little shit. That thought might have gone through Sarah's mind as she learned a lesson about trust and predicting behavior. *Apparently, I've gotten too trusting.* Sarah marveled at how one minute, Jazabel could be one of the best behaving students, and the next minute, she was on the run.

This behavior of Jazabel required Sarah to submit extra paperwork for the system. One of the things both Sarah and Jazabel had in common was hating paperwork. Sarah was always too wordy in her reports. Writing about the day at the rescue ranch, how well her student did, then the incident of the run, Sarah mentioned several times in the report how "good and caring Jazabel was with the animals." Sarah wrote how "diligently Jazabel attended to the chores." She highlighted this student's strengths that day, as she "lived for the horses at the ranch."

The meat of the report was much shorter: "Jazabel left her assigned area of the van and ran." Jazabel was found four days after the run. The following days after returning to school, Jazabel seemed haunted by her time on the run. There were periods throughout the day when Jazabel and her friend would be found skipping classes and sitting together in unsupervised areas, as if consoling or protecting each other from something unknown.

Sarah at first blamed the behavior on the drug use, but later concluded it was not just the drugs. The two girls were the only ones who knew the truth: the secrets of what was going on in that house. Michael's secrets were of sex, drugs, and branding. Still, the young ladies actually thought they were manipulating him by having a free place to get high. His occasional personal request seemed like a small price to pay—or even an honor, since he ran the home with degree of hierarchy.

A dangerous joke on the girls, Michael was using them.

How did this gross predator infiltrate our children's lives? Our children's innocence? Sarah asked herself. Michael had found the weak links: two beautiful young girls who needed to feel important to someone, to find belonging. So many predators had done the same, as Sarah knew all too well. But Michael was really good at it.

Thankfully, Ralph had pushed the tattoo incident, causing the rest of Michael's family to leave the area out of fear of the investigation and what would uncover. As a result, couch-hopping students had one less dangerous place to stay. Otherwise, who knows what would have continued to happen in that home?

As the court proceedings for the tattooing of a minor's private parts dragged on, a plan for some safety for the girls was made between the parents and school staff. Staff was not to let the girls get into any car other than with their parents. Because the center did not have interior locked doors, students could walk outside through side doors but enter only in the front door.

Which might be why Jazabel and her friend could continue to walk off campus to meet cars a few blocks away. They would end up back with their user friends and abusers. The police were called, but nothing happened fast enough to protect Jazabel from her own actions. The school could inform parents or give the girls night-school classes to make up for lost school hours, but eventually Jazabel and Emma would get themselves to where they needed to be, possibly in a locked facility.

Sarah only hoped that something concrete enough was discovered for Michael to be arrested and incarcerated for a long time.

Ralph still had an enormous amount of guilt about the awful father he had been when Jazabel was young and he was an active alcoholic. He did not abandon his children, unlike their mother, but he had only been there physically, not emotionally. He felt so powerless over the past and the chaos it recreated. Jazabel's brother was deep into drugs, and Jazabel was on the same path of risky behavior.

He decided he did not need to feel powerless about this incident with Michael, which is why he reported him for tattooing minors and kept on seeking legal results.

Still, no one was talking to the authority about Michael's use of drugs for sexual favors or what the tattoos meant, especially not Jazabel and Emma. Without enough evidence for any other conviction, the court could only try him for the tattooing private area of a minor.

After a period, Michael's case finally came to a verdict. Michael got a short sentence of less than a year.

These were the events Sarah took home at night, causing her to wonder what was happening to society. *Why wasn't Michael punished more*? was a question she asked in her head over and over, as if she were a justice determinator.

Contrasting thoughts to her questions were swirling in Sarah's mind. Sarah was excellent at understand the opposing side. She knew that second guessing the system would burn her out quickly. Sarah laughed at the vision of herself, robe on, gavel in hand, dealing out justice. What would she do differently? *Law is law*, she thought to herself, as she tried to come to terms with her helplessness in bringing these abusers to justice. *There are always codes, laws, and rights that protect the abuser— but not the innocent.*

CHAPTER 5

After the trial was over, Jazabel was often on the run. She would hang out with her older brother and his friends, doing drugs while being taken advantage of by the older users.

From her perspective, she was having sex with older, cute guys and getting free drugs. A win-win situation, right?

Her behavior of being on the run, not going to school, and drug usage eventually helped her find her way to a residential treatment center. She was given the option of substantial time—18 months—or the completion of a treatment program.

The county worker had a residential treatment center in mind for Jazabel that had an onsite equine training program and an online equine science program. Sarah felt this could be a great place for Jazabel, she could only hope for her success.

Along with Jazabel came her school records, and those records included the learn-and-serve runaway report written by Sarah. The county staff read Sarah's explanation on the wonderful job Jazabel had completed at the rescue ranch, after which, she ran from the social worker during the trip home.

The treatment center placed her into their equine program. They were motivated to see her be successful so they could get approval to further expand their operations.

Because Jazabel was chosen, she was presented with the opportunity to begin her studies to be a horse trainer. She did not hesitate, even though it would take extra classes of horse anatomy and care, because she did not mind working hard on something that mattered to her. She had a love for horses, especially those that needed extra work because of past treatment. Plus, she would graduate from high school with a degree and experience in equine science.

After Jazabel was sent to the residential treatment center, the county had enough reasons to intervene in Emma's life. She was sent home to live with her parents, with the condition of family therapy plus outpatient addiction and mental health treatment. With the court system over her and her parents' support, the intervention resulted in Emma slowly becoming successful at night school.

Signing up to help the horses did not mean Jazabel personally intended to get or stay clean. She could not visualize herself as clean and sober, which she'd consider to be *"boring."* Her first thoughts were about the horses' absolute, unconditional trust. *The horses won't care if I'm high or not*, she told herself. Besides, if she were locked up, getting high would not be an easy possibility.

But the more she worked with horses, the more her vision and goals began to change.

Foremost she needed to complete some seat time. Jazabel sat in her cubicle, diligently studying. She had a goal: if she could work with the horses, she could be independent from her dad, and maybe even society. At that point, she hated most people.

During the initial time at the residential center, she was unable to leave. She needed to move into a higher level of accountability in order to have visitors or family leave time. This restriction formed boundaries for her that, up to this point, no one had been able to set.

Jazabel was unable to spend time with her user friends, but the isolation was not as horrible as she had anticipated. She liked eating and sleeping with a schedule. The regiment was good for her.

Jazabel spent most of her tenth grade and part of her eleventh grade in her lockdown classroom, with her evenings studying back in her room at the residential center. All the facilities were contained in the same building; the classrooms were on the east side, and the residential pods were on the west side of the same floor.

Math was extremely difficult. She had missed many building blocks while using or on the run. There were times she thought her brain was too fried to learn new concepts. As Jazabel remained in the residential center, clean and fed, with each struggle came success. With the successes, Jazabel began understanding the importance of learning.

Eventually, she would finally start training with the horses. The faculty used the large equine barn owned by the local college.

While in high school, she would be able to complete her college equine science degree under two conditions: First, she must become a permanent ward of the county until she turned 18 or finished the program. And second, she must complete the program with absolutely no violations, no warnings—nothing. One strike, and she was out.

She wanted this opportunity of earning the equine degree so badly that she knew she could handle the rules. She used Ralph's guilt to manipulate him into signing the paperwork. "You know it is the best thing you could ever do for me. Just sign me over to the county. You are still my Dad, and I am still your daughter. No damned paperwork will change that." He did it with tears in his eyes, knowing his daughter was right.

As her father continuously improved, Jazabel also started to understand the nature of addiction—including her own. With her brother still on a downhill spiral—asked not to return to the school grounds because of his usage and possible selling—and her mother's whereabouts completely unknown, Jazabel began detaching from her family's problems. Slowly, Jazabel began thinking about her childhood events without hatred. She did not blame her mother or father for her addiction. Jazabel was surrounded by parameters that enforced sobriety, and every day of it made her healthier and stronger.

When she eventually connected with these horses, she demonstrated an almost innate ability to earn respect from them. The staff often noticed her touching her forehead to a horse's forehead, a sign of submission from the animals— and a powerful form of communication between them.

Physical connectedness without strings attached began to feel comfortable for her. She could inhale the horses' warm breath and sense comfort, not fear, as she wrapped her arms around their necks, one after another, building relationships.

Jazabel became a good student. It pleased the staff to witness her success. Plus, there was an additional benefit of strengthening their program, if they could show it was working.

Jazabel had wanted to be an excellent horse trainer, and she owned her accomplishment. It took time, but at the end of her junior year, she finally started training with the horses. The horses brought into the program had often been rescued. In a way, when Jazabel had to detach from seeing her friends and family, these horses started filling the gap.

There was a particularly young filly she worked with that had been rescued out of a junkyard. A sweet animal, she came in dirty and thin—not unlike Jazabel with her drug-yard life. She felt a love for this beautiful animal. This connection was stronger than any relationship she had shared with any other human or animal. Every time they experienced success together, Jazabel gently touched her forehead to the filly's forehead, feeling an overwhelming, warming connection with the pretty little thing. Jazabel taught the filly that coming to her was the safe and easy thing to do. Jazabel would rub the filly's head and all over her body.

Jazabel believed in the gentle horse training methods. She would find a book on the residential library shelf, Neal Davis' *Training Without Fear*. His technique of training without punishment resonated with her. As her only violation, she returned the book, then stole it on another library visit—reading and rereading it.

Someday this little filly will be adopted, Jazabel knew. She wanted the horse to feel confident in her new home. Confidence would create success for the filly, instead of fear creating failure.

She began to realize that she wanted the same for herself. She wanted to be successful in this career of horse training; therefore, she worked hard on her ongoing course work.

The round pen and arena were fabulous for Jazabel. It was in the arena that she could apply her knowledge. In the arena, she did not feel abused or tempted to be the abuser. There, she felt as if she were in control of her actions—not the horses', but her own. Together, they formed a team. She felt power in not being so angry—and in being good at something.

As Jazabel became more involved in her personal and horse training development, she began to understand her life better. She began to understand why consistency was good for horses and children. She became able to assess who was a good person for her and who was not.

Jazabel continued to accept her father with all his faults. She appreciated that he stayed in her life no matter how hard she made it for him to commit to her.

With a light smile on Jazabel's heart, she would often think about the hippie lady. She began to understand that her change began with that lady.

Most importantly, Jazabel's tattoo did not itch much anymore. There were times she forgot she had it. She would never remove it, but it did not have power over her. It was a reminder of her growth.

CHAPTER 6

Today, as many times in her career, Sarah questioned: *How much difference can our public-school system actually make? Potentially what would happen if the public schools were not entrusted to be the whole social service of society? Maybe then, the educational system could actually teach.*

Sarah contemplated how under the current setup, the public school system needed to be the keeper of revolving societal needs, combating so many outside factors: drugs, sexual abuse, addiction, social media, parenting by parents who wanted to be a friend and not a parent, parents who were overworked and tired. In Sarah's mind, public schools could not do it all. Teaching was not just teaching anymore, *but was it ever?* Sarah had to think realistically. Teachers had made lunches for students and kept stoking the rural school furnaces since day one.

Sarah felt that being a school social worker was a large part of who she was. She accepted the fact that she did not *do* social work; she *was* social work. She believed in the ethics of the profession, and that mindset was within her.

But she also knew it was time to retire. She was beginning to question the system in which she worked, the motivation of her students and their parents. But mostly, she questioned her own ability to facilitate change.

She was curious how her retirement would force her to adjust, since being a social worker was completely woven into who she was. She would put the retirement action into motion and figure it out—making it a process, not an event.

The summer that Jazabel was on the run, with school out for the term, Sarah continued to go to the rescue ranch. That summer, Sarah also was a volunteer driver for a church youth group. She did not actually belong to that church, but it gave her an opportunity to be at the rescue ranch and interact with some of her students. Sarah also scheduled time with a trainer. She and the trainer worked with a young horse. Using the Clint Anderson training method, Sarah learned groundwork along with desensitizing.

Through her volunteerism, Sarah also met Dundee, a 25-year-old registered Dunn Quarter Horse. He was considered *a professor*, the kind of horse who taught people to ride.

Ben had accompanied Sarah to the ranch several times. Every time he went, he noticed the overworked staff, the faulty gates, the neglected fences, and their inadequate food and water delivery system. Volunteers struggled with gates or to feed. *That wastes valuable time and energy that could be used on the animals,* Ben thought. Time was a very valuable commodity to him. On more than one occasion, he made a slight adjustment to the weight or angle within a gate's hinge system so it could swing less laboriously, or he would simply move a tank a short distance.

He did not talk about the mismanagement; he simply tried to improve upon it.

Dundee had thrush, which was not unusual for horses in the wet weather, but his was extreme. His hooves were so tender, and they reeked from the smell of rotten yeast. The rescue ranch manager used a holistic approach, which improved his hooves, but then Dundee was put back into the same wet, mucky pen—sinking to his knees in sloppy manure and thick mud. The conditions were red flags for Sarah. Ben felt extreme discomfort leaving an animal there from the first day he went to the ranch. It was difficult for him to watch; he knew the farm was trying to do too much.

Ben was not the only one noticing the conditions. Over time, the rescue ranch manager sensed disapproval coming from more than one direction, and she started tightening up policies. Volunteers and horse fosters were treading softly. Horses were being adopted and moved off the property quickly.

Sarah knew she would follow Dundee to the North Pole. Dundee had been donated to the ranch—old, but in good health. Over the winter, in addition to having problems with his hooves, he was losing weight. *Not good for an older horse*, she thought. So, Ben and Sarah decided to adopt him, a decision that would change Sarah's life course.

The act of rescuing a horse was a real commitment. Upon adoption, as usual, Ben kicked into action mode and immediately started developing a plan for transportation and boarding. He was pragmatic.

Sarah tried to follow all the policies and procedures without causing any reaction from those with power, potentially triggering a non-approval for taking Dundee home. Ben paid an outrageously high adoption fee as a gift to Sarah.

"I want Dundee out of there and at my farm," he said.

Sarah did what she could, but she never could have accomplished any of it without Ben.

Finally, everything was completed, and Dundee was brought to Ben's farm. *Hey Buddy*, she whispered in her horse's ear that night. *I promise you will never have to deal with extreme conditions again—no more thrush.* Dundee rose his head as if to say, "I got it," then went back to munching the high-quality hay she had served him in the corner of his soft, dry paddock.

Ben's farm was not a perfect setting for the horse, but the two continued to work on moving a shed and increasing pastureland. Sarah and Ben did the astronomical job of moving a grain bin from down the road and transforming it into a horse shed, among other endeavors. With Ben's instructions, they used two forklifts to elevate the building onto a flatbed. Solving problems in real time as they developed, they used logs to roll the building onto the truck.

"My idea!" Sarah said, pointing to herself when it worked, as she beamed and basked in pride. Ben nodded his approval and smiled back. But then came the feat of transporting it 1 1/2 miles down the road to the farm— without a permit, of course.

The completed manual labor jobs gave Sarah the tangible reward she needed at that time in her life. A shed in the horse yard—done, completed, crossed off the list!

Levi, Sarah's son, helped dig the corner post holes for the fence. Ben borrowed an old hydraulic digger. Sarah was sure one of them, Levi or herself, would lose a finger, but all 20 remained after the post holes were dug.

Levi had a sharp mind, which compensated for the lack of mechanical direction received while growing up in their female-headed household.

Water needed to be trenched, so Ben borrowed a small trencher. The telephone line was accidentally cut in the process, but at least they had a waterline in place for the horse. Ben wired the building. Sarah helped cover the water line with dirt. Ben had the skill set; Sarah had the dream.

When it came to gardening or tending the animals, she revisited her youth to pull information she needed to be successful. She convinced Ben that composting was beneficial for the garden. Dundee became an asset in that department, as they piled his manure in heaps to age before using in the vegetable beds.

One of the most dominant issues for Dundee's well-being was companionship. Dundee had always been with another horse. Eventually, through several circumstances, Dundee no longer had to be alone. June was bought and made her way to Ben's farm as Dundee's companion. June was a beautiful, Polish Arabian mare, and she knew it. She had a strawberry flea tick on her white coat, offset by a dark mane and black points at the tips of each ear, on her nose, on her tail, and on her legs.

June had the "me first" attitude of a lead mare. June's bloodline consisted of Bandola, a horse once known as "The Queen of Poland." Dundee was happy to have June's company. He tolerated her youth and ego; she returned companionship and leadership to him.

CHAPTER 7

Sarah was still working, but retirement was only a few months away. Sarah stood in front of her mirror, getting ready for work. While brushing her hair, she was listening to the morning news.

Another school shooting in the United States. This time, 10 are dead. What happened to humanity? Why are children shooting children? she pondered as she rushed about, getting ready. She had not totally given up on humanity, but sometimes it was difficult not to feel tainted. Discouraged, she acknowledged that she had seen and heard too much at work and must retire before she became a bitter, old lady.

Do I want to leave still loving my students and their innocence, their curiosity for knowledge—or leave totally feeling hopeless? She was many decades older than them. At times, she felt more innocent than her students, plus more curious for knowledge.

Her desire to leave work did not develop suddenly. She always had the drive to work. She became a school social worker for many reasons: her love of children, her need for justice. Working at the school allowed Sarah to stay at home with her own children in the summers. For a while, that worked, until she started working summer school for more money.

She had been a working mom most of her children's lives, and it had taken a toll on her family. Now she had grandchildren. She wanted the freedom to see her adult children and grandchildren and spend time with her animals. She wanted to enjoy her personal interests at *Sarah's liberty*—a time not dictated by anyone or anything else other than what she felt free to do.

Sarah wanted to adjust to letting go of the concepts, people, and duties that had been very important to her in her career. She wanted to leave her position, giving the newly hired social worker the lateral ability to define the position without Sarah's biases or ingrained habits. Sarah felt she could not be too involved during the transition.

But stepping back left a void in her. She needed to learn to back away from years of dedication and fill that gap with new interests and adventures.

CHAPTER 8

That evening, Sarah drove out to Ben's farm after work. She wanted to touch base with Ben with a quick kiss, then have some time with June before dark.

June was coming along nicely, and Sarah looked forward to the time spent with her horse. Sarah was working on becoming a riding team with June. Sarah had ridden as a child, so she had some experience but still had a lot to learn. Her time at the rescue ranch did not help her in the saddle, as she was mainly caring for the animals or having lessons in groundwork.

Ben filled a role of encouragement in Sarah's life. He was always positive about her interests—with her work, her idea of retirement, and eventually her time with the horses. Secretly, he enjoyed having new animals on the farm. Each step of their lives together brought another project or new learning curve. Retirement was unfolding very naturally. When the office door was closed for the last time, he hoped that Sarah's new life would be busy with meaningful activities.

Shortly after retirement, Sarah was anxious to move to the farm and end her commute to Ben and the horses.

Ben continued as a workaholic. For Sarah, moving in with him meant an ongoing journey of doing things on her own. Sometimes Sarah questioned where she stood with Ben. The back burner was cold and lonely, not that she had not always been independent. Sarah usually had children or grandchildren to tag along with her. Now on the farm and finally retired, she had a different—far different—schedule than most of her friends and family. So, when Ben was either working, flying, in the shop, or spending time with his volunteer commitments, Sarah decided not to wait for her retired life to begin. She would proceed on her own adventures, sometimes with Ben, sometimes without.

Ben is difficult to figure out, Sarah thought. Even with his constantly busy mind thinking about his next project, he would worry about Sarah's safety. She knew that. Ben often worked near the horse shed when Sarah was riding, just to be there for her. But when given an opportunity to travel, he had no inner conflict. When he put activities in his continuum of importance, Sarah was not always on the strong side of the continuum. His compartmental thinking made sense to him, but it gave companionship a different definition than Sarah had held before meeting Ben.

Sarah knew that Ben loved her dearly, but sometimes she longed for more of his attention.

Amid figuring out her life, after Sarah's official retirement date, she started to work with June more intently. Her students' stories were still residing in her memory, at times knocking to be let out. At times, the knock came with a news release of an overdose or arrest. Despite her efforts to shut the thoughts out, Sarah felt sadness that some of the behaviors of her students' families seemed not to change.

Change, to her, was the answer to many emotional and social problems; but change was difficult in patterns of addiction and abuse.

Sometimes the knocks were more pleasant: an ex-student working at the clinic or seen at a public event.

Sarah began to connect with June more and more. She thought everything was going so well. Her time spent with her mare soothed her. June would meet Sarah anytime Sarah walked out to the pasture. "Good morning, pretty lady," Sarah acknowledged June's presence. Sarah gently patted June's nose in long strokes before slipping her halter and lead rope on. June stood contently as Sarah saddled her.

It was an interesting barnyard for riding and keeping horses. The barnyard was a conversion of several acres of crop land that were squared off by two grassy landing strips for the airplanes—one going north and south, the other going east and west. Ben could land a plane on either one, depending on the wind. The strip going east and west was bordered by train tracks. As Ben would take off with his small planes, he noticed it did not take long before the two horses did not bother to lift their heads from grazing. The strips also worked well for short rides.

Sarah mounted June, warmed her up, and moved on to training exercises. She worked on transitioning her from walk to trot while maneuvering through patterns. Sarah cued June to trot, which she responded to smoothly. Sarah decided to slow June down and walk around obstacles. June completed the first three well, but then she started side stepping away from one of the cones. Sarah used rein and leg signals, attempting to redirect June. June grew more agitated and unwilling to move forward in the desired direction. Eventually, she bucked to show her rebellion, or maybe confusion.

Maybe Sarah's lack of skill confused June. One moment, Sarah thought she was staying in the saddle. The next second, she was looking down at the ground, eventually landing flat on her back on the other side of June.

Sarah was thankful she just had the wind knocked out of her and was sore—but did not break anything. She knew the accident was basically her fault. Experiencing the buck caused Sarah to lose her confidence. After that point, she did not hold June to the degree that she should have, and June knew it, capitalizing on that weakness to react more strongly.

Ben observed the change in Sarah, which resulted in June's behavior changing also. He did not want Sarah to lose her enjoyment of the horses. He saw this as a perfect opportunity for a gift.

"For your birthday, I'd like to pay for you to have a trainer for June, to work with both of you," he told her.

Sarah was thrilled at the gift, but finding a trainer was not easy. Sarah spent most of the winter trying to find trainers by reaching out to other horse people for recommendations. Few trainers were available in their area. Nothing materialized that winter.

The next spring, Sarah went to the spring horse auction. The scene reminded Sarah of her childhood livestock sale adventures with her dad. Those days had been spent eating sloppy joes and watching the livestock move through the ring. Occasionally, there was a box of puppies being given away that she got to ogle over and pet. She never was given permission to take one home, but her dad always granted her time to give them some love.

This spring, Sarah enjoyed looking at the horses and talking with the old cowboys in the crowd. While sitting in the crowd, Sarah thought she recognized somebody across the room. *Could it be Jazabel?* Sarah had not seen Jazabel for more than a couple of years, but she could not mistake her long, beautiful hair for anyone else's.

Stunned at how healthy Jazabel looked, Sarah just had to go over and see how she was doing. Sarah knew it was inappropriate to walk up to a student without the student giving the first acknowledgment, but Sarah no longer worked at the school, nor did she have to follow social work protocol in retirement. Sarah was so curious about how Jazabel's life had gone; neither ethics nor the fear that Jazabel may swear at her would stop her. *Jazabel may still blame me for being sent to detention*, Sarah thought, *but I need to know how she is.*

Sarah walked towards her former student and stopped a few feet away.

"How are you doing, Jazabel?" asked Sarah.

Jazabel shot Sarah a confused look, then answered with, "Hi, Sarah," with her well-practiced "I do not give a damn" look.

But Jazabel's eyes softened quickly. She was happy to see her old school social worker, but she still did not totally trust that Sarah genuinely cared about her with no ulterior motive.

"I didn't expect to see you here!" Sarah responded as more of a question than a statement.

"I'm here with a buyer. I'm working as her horse trainer," Jazabel added. "She wants a barrel racing horse for her daughter, and she asked me to help her find a good one."

"Good for you!" Sarah responded, then proceeded as if Jazabel also wanted to know why she was there. "I was bucked off my horse late last fall. It scared me enough that I haven't been back on the horse since. I realized I need help, so I'm looking for a trainer. I figured coming to where the horses are might help me find someone to train mine!"

"I have to tell you, Sarah; without you knowing this, you got me started in the horse training business. I never could have done it without the connections you made for me."

"And she is a real good trainer," a female voice responded, sidling up to them. Jazabel explained to her client how Sarah's learn-and-serve project had sparked her interest, then Sarah's paperwork sent to the juvenile center resulted in getting Jazabel placed in the equine program. It was apparent that the buyer was fully informed about Jazabel's past; none of the information Jazabel was sharing surprised her.

Sarah took a moment to reflect on what she was seeing. She didn't typically follow a student's progress after the student left the area learning center. Sarah believed the students needed to close that chapter of their lives and move on, which meant without Sarah. Sarah cared but did not allow herself the indulgence of being involved.

But at this moment, she grasped how well Jazabel was doing, and how she had carved a career out of her opportunities. *Jazabel took that fork in the road that so many people miss seeing,* Sarah thought.

"I need to thank you, Sarah. What you did for me was the beginning of the change of my life."

"Jazabel, you did all the hard work, but you are welcome. May I use your gratitude to have you say yes to my request to train June and me? Do you have time to work with us? I think I have more to learn than my horse! ...She's an Arabian mare with an attitude. Do you have experience with Arabians?"

"One of my first horses I trained at the detention center was an Arabian filly. I truly enjoyed her, so I focused on Arabians for a while. I can make time."

Sarah smiled with satisfaction, and not just because she had found a trainer. She was ecstatic to see her former student seemingly doing so well.

Jazabel turned to her client who still stood nearby, looking at her to make sure she approved of her spending time training another horse and rider.

"You can use my indoor arena," she approved, "as long as you muck after you're done with the lesson."

Jazabel and Sarah's life together had come full circle. Jazabel would now become the teacher. They both felt their growth, although Jazabel was more apprehensive than

Sarah. She could use the extra money, but she gave herself permission to become "too busy to add a new student horse and rider" to her schedule if she later decided against it. Jazabel felt comfortable planning a way out of a relationship if she needed to. It was her way of not getting too close to people. *People are difficult,* she told herself. Despite her progress, she still struggled.

They exchanged telephone numbers and would decide on the training details later.

As Sarah sat down, Jazabel laughed to herself. *Sarah is still kind of strange,* she lamented, *and still has no sense of style.*

Jazabel took a moment to explain Sarah to her client... her quirks and how she had helped Sarah in the past. She realized everything she said about the lady was positive, as she spoke with a sense of humor and gratitude.

After returning to the ranch, Jazabel thought about Sarah. *Sarah gave me a chance. I owe her a chance*, she told herself, picking up the phone. They scheduled lessons for mid-summer. June would stay at the stables where Jazabel worked, and Sarah would come for lessons. First, Sarah would ride the lesson horses, then she would ride June.

Ben drove June the 25 miles to where she would be boarded for the month. Sarah told Jazabel about June's favorite treats and where she liked to be stroked. As they went through the list that would make the stay more comfortable for the mare, Sarah felt more like a mother dropping off her child at summer camp than a horse owner. Ben and Sarah drove away with the hope June would get the most out of her lessons.

Jazabel put time into June every day. The young trainer got up at dawn and worked with her training horses before the heat, flies, and lesson riders came for the day.

Jazabel was a good trainer, and June was a good student—although it took June a couple of weeks to settle down and let go of old habits. On the other hand, Sarah struggled but improved slowly. Sarah needed to talk to herself to remember the four points of communication. She needed to use her forearm to pull the rein, roll her leg, use her voice, and balance her body. Sarah would go home and practice on a yoga ball.

Jazabel noticed that Sarah had aged and become less fluid but observed her trying hard to be a good rider for June. Sarah had her natural horsemanship biases. Sarah did not like organized sports immensely—or any horse sports that overworked the animal's body, causing injury through continuous use. She also was not fond of using a bit. She had ridden an old Quarter Horse when she was younger. She would tie bailing twine to the halter, and off the two of them would go. She preferred to use a hackamore (with no bit in the mouth) or a side-pull halter. Her horses were ridden Western style.

Jazabel listened intently with a non-judgmental approach, thinking it was comparable to Sarah's approach to people. She did what was best for June and tried to fit Sarah's ability and personality into the training.

Because June was such a pleaser and Sarah was determined to be a good rider, lessons were going reasonably well. Although Sarah seemed to take extra time t o create muscle memory. Jazabel thought if the lesson ended with all the cues and posture done right, muscle memory would eventually kick in. But Sarah seemed to have rigor mortis in her muscles from years of improper riding, making some of the same mistakes over and over, frustrating everyone.

Sarah felt like a slow learner. But finally, after weeks of work, the three were working together better. Not great, but better. The bucking ended after the first few weeks, probably because Sarah learned how to transition from walk, trot, and canter.

Occasionally after lessons and attending to June, Jazabel would open up. Jazabel did not want her past to define her, but because Sarah knew her "then," Jazabel felt more comfortable talking to her about her journey—mostly how horse training had virtually saved her. It was so easy for Sarah to see Jazabel's connection to the horses. Jazabel thought about Sarah, how many times they had discussed Jazabel's need to change her behavior. In those days of adolescence, she would walk out of Sarah's office with positive determination, then meet another user, forgetting about change as the cycle began again.

Jazabel thought Sarah must feel as she had years ago—unsure whether she was getting it right. Just change your opinion about your riding. Sarah, you are a good rider. Sarah did not feel it yet. It would take seeing more success to prove to her that she was doing things right.

Jazabel, Sarah, and Ben's relationship grew closer over time. At first, Ben saw Jazabel only as an ex-user. He was unable to trust her and did not like the time Sarah spent with her. In Ben's mind, druggies mistreated everything around them, especially generous people.

Ben worried about Sarah. He worried Jazabel would take Sarah for everything she could. Ben knew Sarah had put her fate into Jazabel's hands, and he had concerns that Jazabel did not have the knowledge base to train June. He was afraid Sarah would get back in the saddle and get bucked off again, but this time she may really get hurt.

Ben, with his reservations, was polite, and eventually Jazabel won him over with her dedication to work and amazing ability with horses. When it came to training, Jazabel was a workaholic, which was dear to Ben's heart.

What a handsome older man, Jazabel admired, thinking that Sarah and Ben made a sweet couple. As she watched Sarah ride, she realized that Sarah demonstrated more drive and personality than Jazabel had realized years ago. Sarah had a consistent, calm way about her.

In the past, Sarah had consistently chipped away at Jazabel's exterior without being intrusive. *I bet she knew more than I realized about what I was up to at school,* Jazabel realized as she watched Sarah's awareness of the horses and patience with learning a new skill. Jazabel realized Sarah could see through her own behavior years ago. She had known what Jazabel was capable of, even when she was not demonstrating it.

Jazabel secretly felt grateful for Sarah, who had never given up on her. Without Sarah taking her to the rescue ranch, she would not have found her dream career. She would probably have no career; horses had saved her. Sarah had been the foundation of Jazabel's path.

Whether it was their long relationship or their personalities, Jazabel could be brutally honest with Sarah about her abilities but still push her with June. Sarah kept trying. Jazabel thought June had more skills being a partner with a rider than Sarah had as a partner with a horse. Sarah's saving grace was her deep feeling for the horse, and it was easy to see June cared for Sarah, too.

"Up and out with the rein. If you hold the rein too low, June will be confused. *Whoa* is your emergency brake; it means *stop*. Don't worry, Sarah. June will take care of you."

Jazabel did wonder why it took Sarah so long to be an unconsciously competent rider. The muscle memory just did not kick in, but Sarah was getting older. Sarah had a good seat. She was balanced in the saddle, but remembering to hold her reins correctly or at what angle to have her hands while turning was difficult for Sarah.

Finally, Sarah began to correct her own mistakes instead of repeating them over and over again. *Victory!* thought Jazabel. Sarah would tell herself to hitchhike to the right when wanting to turn right. Her hand would go up as if catching a ride. *Oh my god, hippie lady, you got it,* is what Jazabel thought, yet what she hoped to say was, "Good job, Sarah."

The day that "hippie lady," slipped out, Sarah laughed and said, "I knew you were thinking it; thank you for the compliment. On riding, that is."

CHAPTER 9

One rare evening when Jazabel was done with her initial round of training at the barn and was free for the rest of the evening, she went out to Ben's farm for dinner. Driving into Ben's farm was a new experience for Jazabel. She drove in her 2006 Ford 150 4x4 pickup. As she pulled in and parked near the house, she saw three airplanes on the property, two sitting in the yard, and the third sitting half out of a hanger. Trucks and truck parts were skewed around the shop yard. Ben's personal and professional, busy lifestyle materialized right before her eyes.

As Sarah walked up to the pickup to greet her, she noticed how clean it appeared. *Jazabel still needs to control what she can, and a clean, damn, pickup could be controlled*, thought Sarah.

"Hi! I like your rig! It even has a hitch!" shouted Sarah, a little too loudly.

"Yes, I am ready to pull a horse trailer at any time."

Sarah and Jazabel walked around the house to the back. June and Dundee were in an electric-wired, fenced area beyond the house. And in that fenced area was a wood-grained horse shed. It was clear to Jazabel that June was enjoying being back at home.

Sarah's garden extended right next to the fence. Nothing really defined Sarah in this period of her life more than her garden and the horses. Her kids were off carving out their lives as they should be, while she nurtured the life on this property. She created the abstract element of the farm, this feeling of being welcomed.

Sarah and Jazabel made small talk while walking around the farm before finally coming inside for dinner. Sarah had taken care to have everything clean and near perfection for Jazabel. Jazabel had told Sarah she like peppers and shrimp. So, Sarah had run with it. Using garden produce of peppers and onions, Sarah made shrimp fajitas for dinner.

"You're fussing too much," Ben had told her. "It is just a meal," But Sarah wanted to do this for Jazabel.

"She's given me so much," Sarah explained. "She deserves to be treated as special as she is."

Given, thought Ben, *we paid her.*

At dinner, Jazabel asked about the airplanes. Ben began to relax and open up to their guest. He was a flight instructor and had been flying since college. He explained the red airplane was a Cessna 182. Ben used it for longer trips. "It goes faster and climbs better," he explained. The smaller, yellow airplane was a Cessna 172, which he used for training flight students. The older airplane in the hanger, a Taylor Craft, was built the same year Ben was born. He bought it, because it took more skill to fly. "It is an excellent stick and rudder," explained Ben. "It is not equipped with a lot of instruments. While flying it, pilots can learn the feel of the airplane instead relying on the instruments."

Ken was a First Lieutenant in the Civil Air Patrol. "Sarah belonged to the CAP for a while," Ben explained, "but her favorite member died, and the whole CAP was too military for her."

See? The lady still has a little bit of down-home, country/hippie girl, resist-the-establishment in her, Jazabel thought.

Ben and Sarah would personally compete for ranks in the CAP. Her formal education gave her an edge; Ben's Aircraft Licenses and Pilots Association standing brought his rank up.

Jazabel watched them interact over dinner and understood what Sarah saw in Ben. He seemed to take on life with a vigor. Ben had been involved in many business adventures, not always successful. But even if he experienced failure, he was not discouraged from trying his next idea.

Jazabel felt oddly surprised that Sarah's life was so adventurous. *The hippie lady has lived,* she thought. Jazabel recognized that her partner was confident. She thought it must be hard for him to be humble when he had mastered so many interests. But Sarah could stand on her own merit, something Jazabel had not fully appreciated until now. Sarah had left a dysfunctional marriage, raised her children, and earned her master's.

Jazabel had not had the ideal picture of childhood either, but she could see how even dysfunction could transform into something that made sense and helped her thrive. Ben and Sarah complemented each other. They were two pieces in a puzzle that included many lives, creating a blended family which included Dundee, June, and now Jazabel. Being a part of this family brought unfamiliar yet welcome emotions to Jazabel.

"So, what do you see yourself doing, now that your riding is coming along?" asked Jazabel.

"My dream is to enter an endurance race," Sarah responded, her eyes twinkling. "Not to race necessarily, but to give it a try." Jazabel saw Sarah look down and sensed she was giving up the dream for some reason. "But I don't know," Sarah added. "I am getting a bit old for that."

Jazabel did not want to see Sarah give up because of her age. She knew that Sarah's age was still just a mindset; as soon as Sarah thought she was too old, she would be too old. *Baby steps, one day at a time*, Jazabel thought, considering how Sarah might be able to work towards a race.

"You could participate in a Minnesota nature ride," Jazabel suggested. "It's not an endurance race but it is a two-day ride, around 30 miles. The one night you spend out is at an off-the-grid type camp. The package includes a bunk for the rider and a stall for the horse." Jazabel explained how the adventure would be an excellent start for Sarah and June to become comfortable riding in a group, plus the pace would be slow. Riders were encouraged to bring cameras, because the local vegetation would be identified—including flowers, ferns, mushrooms, and other fungi.

The idea eased Ben of his anxiety. He believed Sarah had high potential to get hurt if she started out too vigorously on her dream. Not that he did not want her to go after it, but he wanted her to use caution.

Sarah lit up at the idea. *This is something I could do*, she thought to herself as Jazabel explained the ride.

"Sarah, here is the website. You have to register quickly, because the deadline is close," informed Jazabel. She told Sarah she would not be able to go with her, but she would help prepare June and Sarah. Jazabel added, "You two will be fine, and the experience will be good for both of you."

"I can schedule the shared horse trailer from Curtis and drive the two of you," Ben offered. He went on to explain that Curtis had been his neighbor for as long as he could remember. Sarah got interested in horses about the same time Curtis's children did. So, they decided to share the cost and buy a horse trailer together.

Ever since Sarah had retired, she felt she was outside her learning curve, or at least like she was adding another factor to it. *This trail ride should be fine*, she reassured herself. *I love flowers, photography, and June. What could go wrong? Besides, Ben and Jazabel are backing me.*

Jazabel left the farm later than she had planned. "Sarah, thank you for the wonderful meal," Jazabel said, as she was thinking Sarah always tried too hard. Jazabel reflected on how everything had tasted very fresh and delicious. Sarah had tried hard, because she valued Jazabel's existence. Sarah wanted Jazabel to feel how absolutely wonderful she was. And Jazabel did feel good.

As she drove off, Jazabel thought how Sarah was a bit odd, but *in a good way.* Sarah had seemed a touch clumsy in the kitchen. *Maybe that is her issue with riding; she's naturally clumsy.*

After Jazabel's car lights disappeared down the driveway, Sarah immediately registered for the wilderness ride.

CHAPTER 10

With June back at the farm, they began their training for the wilderness ride immediately. Jazabel mapped out short trails in the area, which required a short trailer ride. Fortunately, Sarah and June were becoming pros at loading the trailer.

After loading, they headed off to Jazabel's. With Jazabel's assistance, her horse, Tank, or another horse was loaded. Jazabel and Sarah would trail ride in many different locations to develop confidence with the different terrains. The experience was great for both Sarah and June.

Additionally, it was great for Jazabel. She was able to trail ride without the expense. Sarah covered the gas and any other costs. It was a win-win situation.

The two would bring packed lunches or dinners. They would stop, relax, and talk. Occasionally, they met other horse people. They mentored each other: interpersonal development for Jazabel and horsemanship for Sarah. Jazabel benefited from having an older woman as a friend. Sarah was not her mother, but she could answer questions about topics that covered feminine experiences.

Still, only her mother could answer her questions about her childhood experiences.

Occasionally, Jazabel would mention a boyfriend. She would feel uncomfortable if her boyfriend would push too hard or be too kind and thoughtful.

"The bad boy is familiar to you," Sarah mentioned. "You likely find it natural but run from that familiarity—or in your case, get on Tank and gallop!" They shared a laugh before Sarah continued with a suggestion. "When someone is thoughtful and kind, just sit in the moment for a while and get used to it—like Tank's gas!"

Sarah knew how to mix the right amount of humor into their serious discussions and bring it back to the horses in a way that made it easier for Jazabel to listen and reflect. They both laughed.

Jazabel was growing, but so was Sarah. Riding confidence was a true personal growth point for Sarah.

One trail they rode on was physically closer to the wilderness trail ride. The intention was to get them used to similar terrain so that there would be no major surprises on the day of the ride. On this trail, there were streams to cross and dense trees to maneuver through. Each new obstacle brought an opportunity for June to resist and spook—or trust Sarah and inch her way through.

June and Sarah handled the trees quite well, slowly bending around them to follow the course. The goal was not to go so close that Sarah's legs would get scraped. This precision required that June listen to Sarah's cues and respond in the moment.

When it came to the stream, June hesitated. Then she over jumped the stream—a common practice by a horse learning to jump something new.

"Whoa!" Sarah exclaimed, thrown to the side as June attempted to trot away from the stream. Eventually, Sarah pulled herself back to the center of the saddle and brought June to a halt. Sarah stayed on, but it was not pretty or close to eloquent. Jazabel knew this would be a problem when Sarah and June were out alone.

"The best way to get her used to the streams is to practice them again," Jazabel coached. "Let's do it now."

Sarah turned June around, as the horse's ears perked and nostrils flared at the idea of going over that running water again.

"Turn June back and forth as you approach the stream, so she does not fixate on the stream. I can tell she is interested in crossing, but you have to help her learn how." When June made a small move forward in the right direction, Sarah was to reward June by taking the pressure off her reins, as long as she did not try to turn away from the stream.

They worked on this skill for over an hour, but when the lesson was done, both June and Sarah were relaxed going across the stream. Headed back to the trailer, they traveled on a prairie dirt road. Jazabel rode beside Sarah and June.

"I want you to trot, then when you are ready, lope June." She sensed Sarah still feared being bucked off when transitioning into a lope. *She must get over it. But in her own time*, Jazabel thought.

Sarah trotted June, then just before loping, she slowed her down.

"That is okay; whenever you are ready." After the third try, Sarah allowed June to lift into a lope.

"Yay!" Jazabel encouraged. "You two did it on the trail, not in the arena! June did not buck, and you lifted into the lope! Beautiful! You are ready, Sarah."

And they were.

The rest of the walk to the trailer, Sarah beamed. Jazabel felt proud of both June and Sarah.

CHAPTER 11

About a week before the trail ride, Ben realized he had planned to fly to Montana with his son on the same day of the trail ride. He was angry at himself for not attending to the details, although he could not change either date.

"I will help you get the trailer and load June, but after that, I'll need to take off. I know you will have plenty of support," Ben reasoned. "I can't wait to hear all about the adventure later." His words were genuine. It would be fun to hear her story.

As the scheduled tasks were developing the day of the ride, Ben had filled his day too full. He had organized his trip as well as he could possibly, but the airplane was left at the airport in town instead of on the farm, and unfriendly flying weather was moving in. His morning was jammed full of telephone calls between his son and the National Weather Service. He had to leave the farm before the horse trailer was even in the yard, resulting in June not being loaded as he had promised Sarah.

"I have to leave now," Ben said in a matter of fact tone.

What could Sarah do besides say, "Okay." She did not want Ben to be in danger by delaying his flight, but she secretly hoped he was torn a little between helping her and getting in the air on time—or maybe at least he felt he was letting her down, even if he could not control the circumstances.

But it was a simple priority based on his experiences; he needed to ensure proper weather for a safe flight. Ben was too practical to worry about Sarah's feelings. It would do no good. How could Sarah argue with that?

The new development did put pressure on her and changed her plans. Knowing things like this happened, she was packed and ready to leave anytime. But her day was off schedule.

"Be sure to report daily on your progress," Ben requested.

Sarah replied, "Of course. I will do my best, but I do not know if I will have service; plus I'm supposed to turn off the phone during the ride." Sarah knew she was not to use her phone for anything but photography on the trail. She hoped she had hidden her slight resentment of being on the bottom of his importance list. She did not want to appear needy, or worse, controlling of Ben's time.

Sarah wished Ben a safe flight and gave him a hug. After calling to check on the weather one more time, Ben left the farm.

After getting into the cab, Sarah noticed that the pickup was nearly out of gas. *Damn*. Sarah would have to pull the trailer into a gas station. She thought about which station on the way was less busy and most easy to maneuver a trailer in and out of.

First things first, the horse trailer was still at Curtis's. Sarah thought she was almost capable of hitching it on her own. But she could only hope she was strong enough to handle popping the ball up and cranking the goose neck onto it. If she dented the trailer or pickup, *so be it,* she told herself. She would do her best not to, but that was all she could expect of herself.

Luckily, it was a nice day, because the air conditioner was out in the pickup. Right now, if Sarah were leaving with June in the trailer, she would arrive at the starting point in plenty of time for registration. But driving over to Curtis's to get the trailer would add 20 minutes onto her route. She calculated that she would come in a little late for registration.

As she turned into his yard, Curtis was waiting for her. Relieved, Sarah knew his strength would greatly assist her in this part of the journey. *Curtis and his wife are good people,* Sarah thought. She was glad to have them in her life.

Curtis was standing by the trailer, waving her into his yard, indicating where to back the pickup. Everything went well with the hook-up.

"Need any help loading June?" Curtis asked.

"No thanks, but that was nice of you to ask," answered Sarah. She had been practicing with June many times over the last few weeks; therefore, she did not foresee needing any help.

"Okay then," he obliged. "Now drive up to my gas tank, and I'll fill up the pickup." He pointed across the way to his farm service tank.

"No Curt, I can't do that."

Curtis replied, "Don't worry, I will charge Ben. Plus, you do not have to worry about flies on June when the trailer is in the gas station. And truly, I wanted to be part of the adventure. Now I can do my part."

"Okay, thank you so much. But make sure you send us a bill for the fuel. Plus some for your time."

What Sarah did not know is that Ben had previously called Curtis and asked him to make sure Sarah got on her way in the least stressful way. Curtis was trying his best to follow Ben's directives.

Curtis had to give her credit for her courage as he actually wished he were going with her. Sarah secretly wished he were too, but she knew she would be alright.

Wow, somehow I might actually be running on time, Sarah thought as she pulled away to load her horse. It was amazing how quickly Curtis had gotten the trailer ready for her.

As she drove back to her pasture, Sarah thought about her beloved horse. She believed June to be a sweetheart. The Arabian blood in her gave June a little extra sweetness and energy, and all the lessons with Jazabel had taught Sarah to be confident and effective with that energy. The experience had calmed June down.

Today, June intuitively seemed to understand that they were on a significant adventure. June trotted towards Sarah, lowering her head to get her halter adjusted. Sarah made sure she had plenty of apple pieces in her pocket as rewards. As Sarah sprayed June for flies and loaded her, Sarah would occasionally treat June with a fruit piece. Sarah liked giving June carrots and apples instead of processed horse treats. The apples June received grew on Ben's tree.

What a beautiful Polish Arabian June is!, thought Sarah as the sleek animal stood beside her. Her white hair with reddish brown flecks glistening in the sun. Sarah had taken extra time to groom June the day before. Amazingly, in the last 12 hours, June had failed to roll in the dirt, her usual pastime. *June seems to want to look her best today,* Sarah considered, uttering a small chuckle.

Every detail besides the trailer not being in the yard was going well. *It was really happening!* Sarah's nerves began to show. She reminded herself to remain calm, so that June did not sense her natural anxiety of running late and her own anticipation and excitement of the ride.

"We are a good team, Juney." Sarah said as she touched her head to June's head, reflecting on the connection with something living that she had observed to be vanishing in today's society. Sarah pondered how children's school days would go better, if only someone, an adult in their lives, had taken a moment to touch the child in a connecting way, head to head like June and Sarah or a simple human hug. She knew she was guilty of sending her own children off to school without connection after a morning of chaos at home, something she felt bad about now.

Sarah's attention shifted back to June. "Let me go grab the food and water supply out of the fridge, and we will be on our way. Oh my, I almost forgot our tack." She placed the freshly cleaned saddle and blanket in the compartment on the right side of the trailer. She grabbed the grooming bucket filled with brushes and fly spray from the shed and added it to the supplies loaded.

Sarah had packed a sandwich for lunch but included her favorite allowed treats of dates and nuts, then of course carrot and apple slices. There would be points along the way to water the horse and consume drinking water for Sarah, but she wanted to bring some of their favorites for their travels. Plus, she knew she would appreciate the convenience of having her own supplies on the ride.

After putting the food in the pickup, she loaded June effortlessly. Off they went with the truck and trailer rattling down the road. Fortunately, it was pavement from the farm to the trail ride. No dust for the team to inhale!

On the drive to the trail ride she called both Ben and Jazabel. She was able to talk to both of them, which was somewhat unusual. Ben was getting familiar utilizing his headpiece, phone, and Bluetooth equipment in the airplane. She assured them both she would group text them right before she hit the trail.

"I'll call the kids for you to let them know you are on the way," he promised. She was grateful he could do that, because she really needed to attend to driving.

CHAPTER 12

Sarah and June drove for three hours without stopping.
Sarah pulled into the registration lot, which was basically
a parking lot full of empty pickups and trailers. Most were
a decade newer than theirs, but that was fine. This rig met
their needs except for lack of air conditioning; open windows
were fine for today. Sarah needed to find an easy parking
spot; she was not great at backing up the gooseneck trailer.

Sarah observed that it seemed weirdly quiet, with no
horse and rider teams in sight. It felt like walking into church
so late that no one else was rushing in.

*Oh my gosh, I missed the instructional piece and the
start of the ride*, Sarah fretted. Before the day of the ride,
Sarah had considered staying overnight in a nearby town
but felt the three-hour drive would be less traumatic for
June than staying in an unknown stable. Staying at home
until the ride meant Sarah and June could relax the night
before in their own pasture and bed.

Moving on from lamenting over being late, Sarah found a spot on the opposite end of the lot. It was perfect, one where she could drive right in and out. Plus, there was a little shade for the trailer.

She got out of the pickup and walked over to the lone man in the lot, who was tearing down the registration table. He seemed intently ready to pack up and leave. He never looked up to catch Sarah's eyes, as she walked towards him.

That did not stop her from explaining and asking the man, "I am running late. May I still please get on the trail ride?"

Brian replied, "Sure, the group only left about a half hour ago. I'm sure you can catch up. But as far as registration goes, my computer couldn't connect out here in the wilderness. I say all that to say, I can help you if you've completed your online registration." Brian said in a no-fuss manner.

"I completed everything online except the registration fee. For some reason, it would not take my card information."

"No problem. We had difficulty accepting credit cards over the internet. Could you write a check?" Sarah was starting to lose patience with both Brian and herself.

"I left my checkbook at home. Now what? I really wanted to do this, and time is passing quickly."

"No faster than normal," Brian said in his steady, slow pattern. "But I get you. Just make a note to yourself to send the check later." Then Brian gave Sarah a piece of paper with the fee amount and address. He assured her that her identification and liability forms should have been filed since she completed them online, but he simply could not double check with his computer down. She indicated to Brian she had not been able to print out her confirmation number, because of the inability to pay with credit card. Brian believed everything would be fine, and paperwork would be at the bunkhouse that night. It really did not matter to him at that point. The paperwork could be completed by pen and paper later. She threw the piece of paper he gave her into the pickup.

Sarah was happy to finish her conversation with Brian, because she was anxious to get June unloaded. Sarah wanted to make sure June was relaxed before she took off on the trail.

Sarah assured herself that her team–with the assistance of Jazabel and tireless practices—was ready for this lone ride, with or without a group of strangers. Jazabel had taken different horses on their practice rides, because she wanted to accustom June to the interactions between the different trail horses. But basically, Tank was Jazabel's ride. He was also Sarah and June's favorite horse partner—a big, old Quarter Horse, tried and true.

On trips near the farm locations and shorter trail rides, Ben and Dundee would go with the other four. Dundee looked to be in better shape than he had been since they rescued him—and quite studly for a 26-year-old gelding.

June backed out of the trailer with ease. Sarah led June around to stretch her legs. June grazed and drank water for a moment while Sarah got the tack out from the trailer and relaxed a moment herself. Sarah did some simple stretches for her own mobility. She brushed June and saddled her up as she reflected. *A big moment with no audience. Our first trail ride together without Jazabel, Ben, or Dundee.* Sarah heard imaginary cheers from a non-existing crowd. *Oh my, we never thought to practice absolute solidarity.* She would not let that worry her, as she completed some simple ground exercises with June. *A quick move of the front quarter, both sides, then move the hind quarters.* Sarah added a few back-up steps, and they were done.

Generally, these larger group trails rides traveled slowly, so Sarah thought they could join the group without overworking June. June was a fast walker. And if they never caught up, *so be it.*

Sarah guessed they could enjoy this part of Minnesota on their own, although Sarah would miss the vegetation information part of the organized trail ride. She had been eager to hear the trail master pointing out the wildflowers and vegetation. Giving the scientific names and explanation of the plants would have been interesting and a learning experience. At the end of the ride, Sarah would have known the properties of the native plants: if they were poisonous or edible, and what their medicinal purposes were. Sarah would never remember the names perfectly. These days she needed more repetition to remember things.

Her favorite plant of northern Minnesota was the wild orchid. She had only seen one once. Sarah was not sure if she would be traveling through the northern orchid's natural habitat. She quickly reflected on June. *Really, plant knowledge is not the priority of today's activity. The priority is our solo ride—the connection of horse, rider, and nature.*

Before getting on the trail, Sarah group texted Jazabel and Ben, and her children. "We are starting the trail. See you in a few days. Dang, I forgot my camera, will use my phone but cannot use it to call or text, plus cannot charge at campsite. If you do not hear from me, all is going well." *Famous last words*, thought Sarah.

She put her phone in her waist pouch, put her backpack loaded with water, dates, nuts and a sandwich on her back, and mounted June. She had chosen not to explain she missed the trail ride and hoped to catch up soon. She thought Ben would think she was complaining. Plus, the information could cause others to stress over nothing. Sarah knew she had this; within an hour, they should be with the group.

Before mounting June, Sarah rubbed the sides of June's face and rested her forehead against June's. "I'm so proud of us, girl," Sarah whispered to June. "Are you ready to have a little adventure?"

Sarah mounted June; she flexed June to the left, reaching down and touching her, then flexed to the right, doing the same thing. *What a good girl!*

CHAPTER 13

The trail appeared at the start to be a 4-wheeler/bike, off-road type, starting on the north end of the parking lot. It was well marked in the beginning with laminated Minnesota Equine Nature Trail signs on trees every 100 yards or so. The path was comparable to the old Sioux bike-line trail Sarah had ridden on so long ago: well groomed, wide enough for two horse teams riding side by side.

It was not the wilderness she had expected: *a little too cultured,* Sarah thought. Sarah tried to keep her mind on the trail, but following the signs and occasional fresh horse manure was making the trail obvious. She had hiked trails that put paint splashes on the trees, which worked well. *But that method was possibly used on more permanent trails,* she concluded.

The singing birds welcomed Sarah's ride with their midmorning melodies. Sarah thought she heard a scarlet tanager. She knew this through an in-depth conversation a student had with her about the difference between the songs of a robin and scarlet tanager. Apparently, the scarlet tanager sings deeper. The conversation had taken the whole lunch hour. Sarah was being polite then, but now the information seemed to have a purpose. *Thank you for the information from that laborious conversation*, Sarah thought. But honestly, it could have been a robin for all Sarah could tell.

There is such a simple beauty in the pine trees, she reflected. June seemed to enjoy the trail also. She appeared to enjoy sniffing the air or horse piles. Reality speaking, Sarah had not seen signs nor evidence of horses being on the trail for the last 15 minutes. She thought she would have caught up to the rest of the riders by now. The trail seemed less kept up or used by humans or horses. It appeared to be more of an animal trail.

Sarah thought she would press ahead, which was what she did. *The riders must be near*, she told herself.

Once Sarah was asked what animal she was most like. She thought herself to be the female bison with snowcapped shoulder pressing ahead in a storm, followed by her three calves. So, press ahead she would do.

At first, Sarah thought maybe the group was riding deep into the woods, with the possibility of a sighting of some unique Minnesota vegetation. The trail was closing in around June and Sarah.

The pine trees were closer, and at times very little sunlight shone on their path.

Sarah kept her mind on the trail but would occasionally take a photo. She realized the phone camera could not capture the beauty and serenity she was experiencing.

Although June and Sarah were alone, the experience was wonderful. The smell of pine filled the air. It was a sweet, pungent smell, unlike any pine scented candle she'd ever smelled, simply unforgettable.

Everything about the pines, the vision, the smell, even the difficulty of the trail was so rewarding. Still, Sarah fought a gut feeling she was on the wrong trail, *if she could call this a trail*. Sarah began to believe she needed to turn June around and backtrack their steps before they were too deep into the cedar pine.

Maybe we missed the trail marking. Sarah was looking for a clearing where she could comfortably turn June around in a small amount of open space. It would not have to be much room, but still, nothing was available.

Scattered, fallen branches crossed the trail. June adjusted her weight slightly and stepped over them. Sarah remembered Jazabel telling her when June stepped over the posts or went around the barrels in the arena to *just think of those objects as if stepping over branches or going around trees.* "It is the same experience to the horse," she had said. "June will be prepared."

With this thought in her mind, Sarah felt her confidence swell. Sarah spoke to June, "What a good girl you are. You are doing a lovely job." It was reassurance for Sarah more so than June.

She noticed they could make a slight right up ahead. If they continued to make slight rights, Sarah should be able to get June back to the groomed trail. If not, at least if they were back on an animal trail, that would be better than their current path.

What Sarah did not realize is the slight rights were moving her into an area of land that had been hit by a tornado the previous year. As they ventured on, uprooted trees left huge holes in the ground, lying in wait for the naïve team. The area ahead looked like an abandoned war zone with its dangerous terrain.

Sarah was losing her confidence in turning right, but her focus shifted to conquering the shallow ravine that June had to jump right ahead. Sarah tried to balance with June's body. "Trust yourself; you have a good seat," Jazabel had repeated to Sarah over and over. Now that became the mantra Sarah repeated to herself.

Sarah posted as June made the jump. Another actual success for June and Sarah.

During Jazabel's training with June, Jazabel and June had been out on the trail riding without buddies. Unlike Sarah, June was familiar with being the lone horse on the trail with her rider. Sarah had not had that experience, but still felt she needed to be the leader of their team. June appeared very experienced with each new obstacle, until they turned a slight right again. June's ear turned forward, as they both heard a distance knocking. *Probably a woodpecker*, thought Sarah.

Come to think about it, Sarah had not heard any other forest noise for a while. It was extremely quiet on the trail.

With the torn down trees and debris, the path opened then enclosed again. Another slight right was accomplished, but the tree enclosed them.

June began to act a little fidgety. She pointed one ear towards Sarah, listening, as Sarah continued to coax June forward. June would stop, and Sarah would talk and cue her forward. This went on for at least 15 minutes.

Swiftly, the mare turned both her ears to point forward, listening for something invisible. Sarah saw all the signs that she should listen to her horse, but she continued to coax June forward.

Sarah could hear Jazabel's words, "Less is better for June." She responded well to the light, correct cues. Always giving her horse verbal cues and releasing pressure slightly, Sarah rewarded June for taking one more step. But Sarah's gut was gnawing at her. *I should be listening to June. We should be a partnership.* June needed to be confident with Sarah's decisions. That gnawing feeling was growing stronger.

I should have turned around sooner after not seeing signs for the trail ride, she chided herself. As Sarah was pondering through her concerns and what ifs, June brought her head straight up, staring ahead. June made an Arabian burgling fear noise through her nose.

Boy, this is not good, thought Sarah. June had never really done this before. "What is the problem here girl? And what is that smell?" Sarah said out loud.

Sarah was trying to calm June by getting her to focus on her rider, when Sarah saw the thing June was bugling about. *Is it a bear?* The creature was straight ahead in the trail, and then all the sudden something was at her side, eye level. Sarah again smelled a gamey odor. June reared once, then tried to turn around. She reared again. Sarah felt herself falling. And that's the last detail she remembered.

CHAPTER 14

A young bigfoot male was standing in front of the horse. He was mesmerized by the closeness of the animal. He had always watched horses from afar. He had only dreamed about the possibility he could spend time with horses.

The bigger, older male grasped the rein and attempted to catch the falling human. No such luck, now he was attempting to calm the horse and prevent the mare from stepping on the human. Which was not as easy as it would seem to be for an 8-foot tall, bigfoot.

The horse reacted with fear from the smell and sight of this enormous beast.

Looking down at the human on the ground, the large creature noticed she had hit her head. Her helmet must have been unattached, because it was at least 10 feet away from her head and the tree her head had hit.

The younger bigfoot clicked something to the older male. The elder clicked back, handing the rein to the younger bigfoot.

The young one tried to communicate with quiet cues and slow body movements that they meant no harm to the horse and her rider. Slowly, the horse understood and stopped fighting the rein.

The bigfoot pair knew they could not leave the situation as it had developed. They had only wanted to turn the horse around and head it back to more groomed trails. The human had continued to move the horse forward, even with the surmountable communication the mare was giving to her.

Humans generally do not respond to subtleties like other creatures naturally do. Maybe we should have growled deeply or thrown down a few more trees. Growling usually sends humans scurrying. Plus, *without the strength to move the trees, she may have given up and turned around.*

The bigfoot pair knew the path the riding team was taking could have led them to major disaster for both human and horse, and they considered how to protect them by diversion. The previous year's tornado had washed the trail out and left a ravine, tearing apart a dwelling the bigfoot family had constructed deep within the cedar swamp. The demolition was probably a fortunate occurrence. Although they missed their dwelling, members of the bigfoot family were confident they had smelled human visitors. It would have been just a few more deer hunting seasons before a bigfoot would have been spotted by humans. Any sighting would bring an aftershock of swarms of researchers. Nature had taken care of their safety by tearing apart their dwelling. The bigfoot family needed to move deeper into the uninhabited area, where they constructed another dwelling.

The uninhabited areas were becoming rare. Humans came into the areas looking for solitude from themselves. This kept the bigfoot group rather busy relocating. For now, the bigfoot pair had simply wanted to redirect the small traveling party to safety, which was one of their sacred purposes. They valued the essence of the horse and human equally.

This beautiful creature needed to be turned around, they thought of June, *because there was grave potential of her breaking a leg—which could mean her life.*

Now a new situation had developed. They could not leave this human unattended. She was breathing but not moving, and it may take her fellow humans too long to find her.

The older bigfoot suggested, through verbal and sign language, they could bring the human and horse back to their currently-used dwelling. It was not the first time this bigfoot had done something as unconventional.

His grandson sensed his grandfather's feeling of obligation to this band of strangers, even if the obligation may add danger to their own lives. Prevention of harm was the service of bigfoot. Generally, it meant redirecting animals and humans to safety. This generally fared to be an easy task. *Too bad this human has injured herself; it complicates our duty,* he thought.

Grandfather had the final decision, and it was to take the human and horse back to their shelter. The younger male wondered what the rest of the family would think of this decision, but they would not argue or debate it; it was not their peaceful way. They would find a solution that kept the family safe from detection—and solve the human and horse dilemma as if it was just another daily problem.

Calming down the mare did not take much. After the initial fear of the unknown, the horse sensed she was not in any danger. The young bigfoot gave her room when she backed away fiercely, then he would take a single step toward the horse, allowing the mare to back up if needed.

Eventually, he was touching the horse.

Unfortunately, the ability to understand their environment and determine when fear was useful was *extremely underdeveloped in humans. The human would probably still be backing up if she had not passed out,* he thought.

The bigfoot party had ventured further than usual from their dwelling. Generally, during the daylight, the bigfoot group did not travel this far, but a storm was brewing, and the two were gathering food. The grandfather enjoyed exploration time with his grandson. He took this opportunity to teach his grandson how to travel undetected by humans during the day. Occasionally, they would break tree branches and lean them against the tree. From the highest point of the tree, they watched the horizon for movement and abnormal coloring. When returning to the ground, Grandfather taught his grandson to use the broken limbs as a step to the ground, which assisted in not leaving a deep footprint by the tree.

Everything they did was about being as visually enmeshed into their environment as possible. When they traveled, they moved through the shade and shadows of the forest as if the darkness created a highway through the landscape. Now both were smack in the middle of another lesson created by the application of the day's events.

What to do with this injured human and horse—while protecting self and nature?

They took the saddle off the horse and left it on the trail. To them, this device was cumbersome and unnecessary for riding, and it may prevent the possibility of traveling swiftly. They also decided to take off the belt pack around the human's waist and hang it on the saddle horn. It looked confining. They did bring the backpack. They could smell the food through the bag and thought it may come in handy.

The four started the lengthy journey back to the bigfoot pair's homelike shelter—the younger male leading the horse and bringing up the rear as the older male carried the motionless human. They moved as quickly as they could, scanning their environment for obstacles as they traveled swiftly.

Because the two bigfoots had traveled way too far this day, the dominant male of the family would not be comfortable with their distance traveled or the guests of the horse and human. But he would nobly handle the situation.

Happily, they had found a late asparagus crop to contribute to the evening meal. The asparagus should delight the family at the shelter, hopefully making their return more of a celebration.

As the four turned a corner in the shadows of the wooded land, the three conscious members of the party heard a yelp. The younger bigfoot handed the rein to his grandfather and went to investigate. He found a young fox entangled in the underbrush.

"What a frightened little guy." The bigfoot sensed the fox's mother was nearby. The bigfoot could smell her and heard a low, concerned growling that discontinued when the mother smelled the bigfoot.

The young bigfoot reached down, slowly making a variety of sounds that calmed the young fox. The young fox was not hurt, just entangled very tightly in the brush. The bigfoot gently tore the brush loose from the fox and sent it on its way to find its mom.

The adolescent bigfoot returned to his traveling party, taking the reins as the squadron quickly began moving again.

The dominant male met the four a few miles from their dwelling. He had been keeping watch for them as he canvassed the pine wooded area. The dominant male was huge, standing more than eight feet tall with a very dark brown, almost black, coat of hair. This male's ability to camouflage with his surroundings was unbeatable. There were many occasions his own father did not realize how close his son was until his son acknowledged himself.

When the grandfather and grandson met the dominant male, the dominant male's first action was to touch his forehead to the older male's, and then to the adolescent's. This was how they showed affection to each other.

Although the dominant male did not inquire, the older male took his time explaining the circumstances. After hearing the events of the day, together they decided to bring the horse to a small meadow a few yards from their dwelling—and the female back to the dwelling, at least until she awoke.

They found it convenient that she was knocked out. It simplified transporting her, plus she would not be able to share with others their location. Because her head trauma did not seem extreme, they were hopeful that with the assistance of the dominant male's mate, the human's stay would not be long.

Once in the dwelling, they laid the human down on the pine needle and bough bed belonging to the two smaller family members. Their bed mat was in the far rear of the dwelling. It would be a simple task to make the children new sleeping mats, preferably a distance away from the human.

The bigfoot family had no idea how this human would react when she was conscious. Humans were known to be hysterically dangerous.

As soon as the human was bought into the dwelling, the visitor enhanced the curiosity of each family member. They were all given a moment to observe the unconscious human. The bigfoot family gazed at the human, somewhat like a human family might observes animals at a county fair's 4-H barn—although the human was not caged as the animals would be at the fair.

The human was different from them. Her skin was thinner; her hair was light in color and texture. She looked frail in every way. The human's bones looked to be thin and vulnerable to breakage.

Many years before, the older bigfoot had a previous occasion to observe a human at close range, but the rest of the family had not. The rare visitor intrigued them.

The two young bigfoots were in awe at the paleness of her skin and her lack of hair. The human was covered with removable, fur-like protection, which they all had observed from a distance on other humans. It was interchangeable; sometimes, it repelled rain, or sometimes on sunny days it was light and colorful. This was nothing the bigfoot family needed. Her feet were protected. The young female bigfoot was tempted to remove the covering and look at her toes, but the adults decided not to disturb her.

The young female was a curious creature, as was the nature of the bigfoot. They were intelligent, with a sense of duty and honor.

Typically, they would only watch humans from afar, never really knowing what to expect. It was common knowledge that humans would strike out with fear. The family had known of a bigfoot that had been fatally wounded by humans. But they enjoyed watching the human's daily routines when they could. Sometimes they mimicked language or played games with humans by moving their belongings around their campsites or making sounds in the night. Occasionally, with purpose they moved humans out of their territory of habitat by stone throwing, growling, or tree clapping.

This bigfoot family was finding an undiscovered, almost magical awe in their new guest. She was older than other humans they observed. The aging process seemed to change the muscular and skeletal makeup of the human.

After the ceremonial display of the guest, the family members were instructed by the female adult to remain quiet and stay away from the pine mat which the human occupied. The children were coached not to respond to any behavior made by the human when she woke up. The human's reaction may be very unpredictable. But for now, they would let her rest.

The adult female bigfoot turned the attention and care of two younger ones over to the grandfather while she breastfed the baby. Once she knew her children were safe and cared for, the female bigfoot took time to examine the human's head. The bump had bled slightly, which was a positive. Bleeding would release the pressure from the head wound. The female was pleased as she examined the area. It did not appear soft and squishy around the skull. These were all good signs that the human had no internal damage, but she would know more when the human was awake.

The female bigfoot thought she would create a poultice of wormwood plant and dirt with clay mixture, forming a sticky property when mixed with water. The mixture with the worm root would repel parasites and soak up the inflammation from the human's head.

Not knowing how much force she could apply to the skull, she delicately handled the human's head. She imagined it was like handling a large egg. The human's head seemed so big compared to her slight body frame.

Humans were far more destructible than bigfoot in so many ways. With a lack of ruggedness, reasoning, and endurance, this human would not last long in any season. Her light skin would burn in the sun; her fine hair could not repel water or keep her warm. *The poor thing, the younger bigfoot children could possibly outrun her.* So much could go wrong with this human, the female bigfoot hoped the human would heal quickly and be on her way. She did not want to be responsible for her physical wellness for long.

After attending to the wound, the mother returned to her children. The grandfather placed the human's supply pack at the end of her pine bough mat, wanting her to have her items near when she awoke.

He watched her sleep, amazed by her courage to be alone with the horse in the woods. When the sun shone through the trees, he thought he had seen her skin glow slightly. He felt a unique wonderment and value in this human. He enjoyed observing her kindly communicating with the horse while riding. Unfortunately, though, she had not listened to the larger animal and simply turned around.

This was the way of bigfoot: they listened and tried to communicate to *all* in nature.

The mare had a beauty also, he thought. Her bright eyes and light hide matched the human's.

After arriving at their dwelling, Grandfather had taken upon himself the responsibility of connecting with the human. He would make sure she understood they meant no harm to her.

The dominant bigfoot and his son turned their attention to the horse. She was a pleasant mare, gaining their trust quickly. Her dark skin under her light-colored coat protected her from sun damage, and her energy level and long legs gave the appearance of health and endurance. The young male told his father how quickly the horse was aware of the bigfoot on the trail and tried to communicate this information to the human. They observed the mare to be smart, strong, and quick. She had traveled successfully through the brush and cedar swamp during the journey to their dwelling.

The dominant bigfoot and his son made a simple fence of branches to hold the animal. It was against their values to contain any animal, but they wanted to return the human and horse somewhat in the same condition they had found them—prior to the human falling off the horse, that is. This meant they would need to be together upon returning, so the bigfoot family would need to keep the horse around.

The horse also would come in handy to carry the human. Hopefully, she would awaken, feel good, and they could be on their way quickly. They did not fear her but felt cautious of her reaction to them. Plus, they wanted her gone before other humans started looking for her making their way into this area.

The adolescent rubbed the horse's face and back, cueing his intelligence and strength to the mare. He walked her around the perimeter of their crude, bigfoot-made fence, so that she could learn her corral. He took time to drink with the horse. He knew the mare was a herd animal. He would try to convey to her that they would be very near and keep her safe during her stay with them.

Her eyes were huge and full of questions. The adolescent would try to ease her anxiety by communicating with simple sounds and body language. The mare received his message and settled into her meadow for the night.

CHAPTER 15

At the same time Sarah was unconscious in the bigfoot dwelling, Ben and his son, Mathew, were leaving North Dakota in the Cessna 182, headed for Montana. Ben was glad he was able to get the early start, because the flight had been so smooth. He looked forward to flying over the mountains with Mathew. There would be patches of trees with an occasional lake and scattering of small towns in his view as he flew over. He hoped they could find an experienced pilot at the aviation safety conference to learn more about flying the mountainous skies. If not, he still had this quality time with his son.

Ben and Mathew would be landing in four hours with plenty of time to set up for the conference. Ben had tried calling Sarah once without any answer. He thought he would let Sarah call him when she was not riding.

Meanwhile, Jazabel was giving an advanced rider a lesson on Tank. He was a broad horse but athletic. She had been relieved to hear from Sarah that morning when she had arrived at the trail. She wondered how the ride was going for Sarah and June.

Sarah seemed far less wordy than normal. Maybe she was in a hurry to get started with the group. Her mind wandered about how the three of them had trained thoroughly, and everything should go well. She hoped Sarah would not hurry—becoming clumsy and causing an unnecessary accident. *The stress around June would not be helpful,* Jazabel thought. *Sarah is a good rider, but she needs to take it easy.*

Knowing she would not probably hear from Sarah again until the end of the ride, Jazabel brought her focus back to her student on Tank.

CHAPTER 16

Sarah woke up with a pounding headache. She touched the back of her head and felt a crusty mass of dried blood, hair, and dirt. It seemed as if she had a compact of plants and mud on her bump that smelled somewhat like menthol.

She tried to figure out where she was and what had happened to her. She remembered being on the trail. She had been riding June. *Wherever am I?*

Suddenly, Sarah felt she was not alone. *Am I hearing some movement?* As Sarah tried to remember what had happened, her eyes adjusted to the darkness of her environment. Sarah attempted to use all her senses to figure out the surroundings. There was a definite smell of cedar and a slight smell she remembered from earlier. Putting her hand down on the surface under her, Sarah touched pine needle bedding.

Sarah looked in astonishment at the woven tree canopy overhead. It seemed almost naturally whimsical with its large, round, organic shape and style. *Where am I? Is it nighttime?* She thought so. *How long have I been out?*

Sarah could smell that animal-like odor again. Not so horrible, but it reminded her of horses on a wet day.

Suddenly she realized she was not alone. She heard the movement and breathing again. Her frightened, widened eyes were naturally dry, and focusing in the darkness was difficult; but slowly she saw images. She spotted a huge shadow in the circular corner.

Oh my god, what is it? Where am I? Wolves in the corner? No, too big. A bear? Is this a den?

She looked back up at the canopy and walls. They seemed constructed with woven trees and branches. *Am I in a deranged man's homemade cabin?* She panicked, looking back at the figure in the corner.

Now she believed the figure was not human, even though the animal was standing on two legs.

Should I run? Can I even stand up? She moved her body back against the tree-woven wall. Fearful, Sarah had to fight this fear. She needed to assess the situation.

Where is the exit? As Sarah looked around, there seemed to be more of these creatures.

Maybe a pack or a group—family possibly—of, of, bigfoot? Not bigfoot! Fear sickened her. Now she was absolutely sure the shadow of a figure in the corner was watching her. The large shoulders and strong, firm chest of this thing caused her to believe it was a male. In his standing position, he seemed taller than any human she had seen. As his board-flat face came into focus, it seemed aged. His hide appeared to be graying, with feathery hair covering most of his body. He did not move; his expressionless eyes began to appear to Sarah. And they were watching her.

More breathing sounds came from other directions. Yes, there were others. *Others, how many?* Her eyes darted to the middle of the dwelling, stopping to focus on the larger beast. Bigger than the huge one in the corner, he looked as if he was in his prime. *Gosh he is big, at least 8 feet tall if not more, huge shoulders...big, big hands and glassy black eyes that are staring at me.*

Can I run? she screamed in her head. She could feel and hear her heart pounding. Sarah did not know if she could stand up, plus she was not seeing an opening to the dwelling. Not only did she not know the extent of her injury, her fear seemed to paralyze her. It encompassed her whole body.

As her eyes darted around the dwelling, searching for an exit in her vision, there appeared to be another possible male about three-quarters the size of the larger male. Sarah guessed he was a younger beast, maybe an adolescent. The younger male seemed so serious at that moment, his eyes fixed on her, but he did not move.

Sitting on the floor were two smaller beasts, maybe children. They did not move; they looked as frightened as she was.

All the bigfoots were sitting or standing motionless, trying to adhere to the directive given to them earlier—the directive of not reacting to the human. It was difficult; by nature, bigfoots were curious, peaceful creatures.

Behind the two young bigfoots sat another bigfoot. Possibly a female, it had breasts. Proportioned to her size, her shoulders seemed smaller than those of the two larger beasts, not that she did not look extremely strong.

Upon her lap cradled a littler bigfoot. The baby turned its head towards Sarah. Its little, egg-shaped face had chubby, baby cheeks displaying a healthy appearance. This baby-like beast was as frightening to Sarah as the larger beast. The baby seemed capable of running at her and swiftly attacking at any moment.

Sarah could visualize it happening; they all could attack at one time, like a pack of wolves. But her fear was unfounded. The baby continued to cling to its mama's arm.

The mother bigfoot, in turn, stared at the human with an intent look of "don't you dare move." She was afraid that at any time, this human could run and attack her family. *Humans were dangerous.*

Sarah observed the bigfoot family to be scattered within their dwelling; but to them, they were close enough to protect each other. The magnificent beasts knew their ability to swiftly and powerfully protect themselves. Nothing would hurt their loved ones, especially this frightened human.

But they must be tranquil unless otherwise required. They had healed many creatures, but they had never hosted an adult human in this dwelling. The mature members of the bigfoot family were trying to get a handle on the human and what risks she brought to the family. *How old was she? Was she stronger than she appeared? Why was she alone on the horse, traveling through the thick pine and underbrush near the dangerous terrain and cedar swamp?* They were not learning anything by staring at the human.

The human sat on the pine bed shaking and crying. For their own safety, they needed to understand this human better. *Was she aggressive? Was she capable of harming them extremely by reacting out of fear?*

The alpha male lumbered over to Sarah. As he moved into her area, his bridged brow and intensely large, dark eyes evoked more fear in Sarah. He smelled her crotch area—a simple technique to determine her age. He grunted a low sound that seemed to vibrate in her ears, while he picked up dirt from the floor and tossed it in the air.

She knew exactly what he was indicating, with the attitude of many males, apparently not just people, His gesture indicated she was an aging woman. She was a dried-up baron; her time had passed. If her smell told him she was incapable of reproducing, Sarah hoped her smell also announced she was too old to eat.

The male then walked over to the older male and ran his hand behind his father's head, leaning into the older male's forehead. The dominant male seemed to communicate a tender emotion with the older male. The older male did not seem phased by the whole declaration of her post, post-menopausal state.

Sarah misunderstood the bigfoots' intention. They had no purpose to shame this human. The two bigfoots were determining her stage of life, with no sexual intentions.

The older male just sat and watched as the performance of her age was laid out to him. He had no reason to disagree, for he had carried the human for miles. She seemed to be aging and very light in bone and muscle.

Sarah had little clue what her body communicated consciously and unconsciously to the bigfoot. But she suspected she was exhibiting extreme fear as she sat curled up against the wood-woven wall—the wall she wished she could evaporate into.

Maybe her fear was her advantage. The bigfoot males determined at this time she was too frightened to be of any danger to them. They thought the best was to leave her alone for a while.

Sarah heard sounds made by the larger bigfoot as they moved away from her. The dwelling seemed to vibrate with every sound made by him, as her fear grew more, if that was possible.

Any more fear, and I may pass out, she realized.

A moment after the male communicated, Sarah saw the group moving into a circle of mixed ages and sizes of bigfoots. This vision shook her belief of reality. The group seemed to be reaching for something, then they began eating. There was no tearing of flesh, just gentle eating. The posture of these beasts was perfect as they sat upright, using their hands for eating berries. They seemed to use their palms instead of their thumbs and fingers.

Sarah took the opportunity of not having their eyes on her to scan her immediate area. At her feet, perched amongst the pine needles, was her backpack containing her water. Suddenly, she felt very thirsty. The day's injury and stress of meeting her captives caused extreme dehydration. She needed desperately to drink.

She held her head and slowly reached for her water. She watched her captives to determine if her movement evoked any aggression in them. None. They continued to eat. Sarah took a couple of small sips, not knowing how long she would be there, therefore not knowing how long she had to make her water last.

Sarah dug for her phone in the backpack, thinking maybe she could call for help. There was no phone in her backpack. *Where is it?* Then she remembered it was in her fanny pack. She reached down for her fanny pack, but it was gone. *Oh no, no phone, no identity information.* She was panicking even worse than before. She heard a terrifying movement again, as the dominant male approached her with something. Sarah curled up by the wall of the shelter as far she could, trying to hide. The bigfoot gingerly put the item down at the foot of her bedding and glided away into the darkness of the shelter. Sarah decided when he was a safe distance away, she would check out the unknown item, which he apparently wanted her to have. Uncontrollably shaking with fear, she waited until he moved back to his seating place.

Suddenly, she was struck with the thought, *there is no safe distance from these enormous animals.* Sarah shook as she deliberately examined the item. *Wild strawberries. Are they a gesture of kindness or a ploy to keep me alive as long as necessary? What to do?* Sarah pondered. Every decision could mean her life.

She concluded she should eat the strawberries so as not to insult the bigfoot host; plus, Sarah needed to keep her strength up. What Sarah did not realize is that her decision to eat or not eat the berries mattered little to the bigfoot. He was simply being kind.

I could manage to force a few berries down, she thought. The berries were small, dark red, and delicious. As she finished them, the breasted bigfoot started walking over to Sarah. Sarah could not only see the female walk towards her; she also felt her force through the vibration under her bedding.

She was not as enormous as Sarah had originally thought, but she still looked forbearing and nefarious. Remaining in the perimeter of the female, the huge male bigfoot hovered.

Are they preparing for the attack? Sarah wondered.

The bigfoot couple cautiously assessed the human's unpredictable behavior. The human looked harmless, but she could injure his mate, and he was the insurance against that. The female bigfoot first sat on the bedding with Sarah's pack between them. She also felt Sarah's shaking through the bedding of pine. The female slowly began to rock her body in a calming fashion with the hope that the human would mimic the movement. Using the pack as a barrier, the female bigfoot slowly inched towards the backpack until she picked it up and placed it behind her. Then the female made cooing and humming sounds, trying to calm Sarah.

The attempts failed. As the female bigfoot inched towards the human, Sarah trembled with fear. *Calming down is impossible at this point*, Sarah thought. *Screaming, thrashing, running aimlessly, now that would be possible.*

The bigfoot gently picked up Sarah's right hand. Watching Sarah's face as she reached the arm high and maneuvered it forwards and backwards, the bigfoot was checking for mobility in the limb and pain in the human's eyes. The female bigfoot had assessed many creatures for injuries; she could recognize pain in any animal's eyes. No pain was visible in the light-colored eyes, only tears of fear and distress.

After she completed the right arm, she did the same thing with the left arm. The female bigfoot reached for the right foot. Sarah gently kicked as an auto-defense mechanism. The female bigfoot held onto the foot and moved with Sarah. With this display of flexibility in the movement of Sarah's foot, the female believed that the right leg and hip were not broken or injured. She checked out the human's left leg, moving it up, down, and around. Next, she firmly held Sarah's shoulders and twisted one way and then another.

Sarah could smell the female; her face was so close. Sarah dared not to stare at the beast directly, as the female moved her hands to Sarah's head and held her chin. She moved Sarah's face to the right, then to the left, while she listened for clicks and looked for lack of mobility. She determined some clicks she heard were due to the age of the human. They were coupled with primal, fearful whimpers, but nothing was broken.

She bent the human's head forward to examine the back of it. As she worked, she continued cooing at Sarah in a reassuring tone. It reminded Sarah of the times when she'd checked out June's hooves, telling June she was a good girl, letting the horse know that everything was okay, and that she meant no harm. But Sarah could not believe these creatures meant no harm.

After checking out the back of Sarah's head, the female bigfoot made eye contact with her and nodded. Sarah finally gained the strength to gaze back into her deep, round black eyes, which pooled with moisture. The bigfoot believed the human was fortunate not to have broken anything. The female bigfoot stood up and left Sarah's space, the male following his mate.

CHAPTER 17

That was terrifying but somewhat painless, Sarah reflected on her experience. Her head was tender, but the bigfoot was careful with her. Sarah was still so frightened she wanted to scream, but something inside told her not to. *Who would hear it anyway?*

Once she was left alone, Sarah felt another urge: to run. In her examination, she established that nothing appeared to be broken. She would run and call out to June as she ran. Hopefully, June would respond, and possibly she would join Sarah. *June is the first horse to meet me in the pasture every day,* Sarah thought, *so this scenario might be possible.*

With every ounce of energy and courage Sarah could muster, she got up, shot past the bigfoot family still sitting on the floor, and ran straight out of the dwelling. The family watched in amazement. She could move out quickly for a fragile human, but where did she think she was going? It was too dark for her to see in the forest, and a storm was moving into the area. No one reacted, as they stayed seated in their circle.

The young ones followed the cue of their parents and did nothing but listen to the silence of the night. Simultaneously, the group heard a thump, then a moan. The three adults looked at each other, and finally the grandfather got up. He would go save the human from herself.

Sarah had run outside, thinking she would be able to see into the night, but it was totally black. The moon and stars were hidden by overcast skies. Sarah made it about 10 feet and tripped over a log, falling flat on her face. Lying there, catching her breath, she turned and looked up. The older bigfoot stood over her. She felt helpless in darkness, as her screams fell as flat as she did in the night. Other than the bigfoot family, only the night and June heard her.

June perked her ears for a moment, then went back to eating. The bigfoot male stood over Sarah. He shook his head in wonderment at her irrationalism. What was she attempting to do? He easily picked the human up, brought her back to the dwelling, and put her down on the pine bedding. He patted her on her trembling head, trying to let the human know everything was okay; she was safe. *Just rest, get well, and let the storm pass.*

Sarah laid on her bed of pine boughs, exhausted from her failed escape. The natural mat was surprisingly comfortable. The pines had a spa effect, with the right aging of the needles making a soft, aromatic bed. It was a contrast to her Christmas tree decorating season, as this time, she was resting on the boughs.

As Sarah was lost in her memory of preparing the Christmas trees for her family, the family of bigfoots had disappeared to their bedded areas in the containment. They retired, not unlike sleepy campers in the darkness of the night, but there was a distinct difference. The dwelling had dark shadows that contained the bigfoot family. They were there, but almost invisible. Slowly in the darkness, her fear and anxiety overcame her, as she felt her vulnerability amongst the bigfoot family. She was alone with these creatures that until then she had not believed to exist, yet she so far had been picked up, smelled, fed berries by, and examined by one or more of them.

I was actually put to bed like a child by a bigfoot, by the monsters of the night! Sarah struggled with this reality. Her overwhelming fear prevented critical thinking. She gave herself the impossible task of not wanting them to sense her fear and anxiety. *Think about your beautiful family*, she told herself. But that created a deep sense of remorseful sadness. Sarah switched her thought process; she had to remain calm. She tried to compare it to working with her horse when she or June felt fear. When June reacted in fear, it created a dangerous situation.

Where is June? Did they hurt her? Would they hurt my horse? She called out to June. All she heard was an occasional sleeping moan and a gruff from one of her captives, but no answer from her horse.

Sadness overwhelmed her every cell. Sarah had long passed feeling fear; she felt terror.

Thinking of her students at risk, she recalled that they were a handful. *Fear* had been their open door to exhibit disruptive behavior, creating a playground of destruction in the classroom. She understood it completely. If a bigfoot felt fear from her, it may actually harm her, or worse, get rid of her by eating her.

Oh my gosh. The thought of being torn apart and eaten one mouthful at a time overwhelmed her. She went as far as creating the sound of crushing bones in her head. *Think, Sarah. Did you see any human bones in their dwelling? No, but they could bury the evidence,"* she argued with herself. *Plus, it was too dark to see details in the shelter.*

Sarah knew this was unhealthy thinking. She kept telling herself to quiet her thoughts. *Breathe, breathe.* She could not think at all, because if she did, she either had thoughts of her family and their faces, possibly never seeing them again, or on the other end of the continuum, thoughts of being raped or eaten by a bigfoot.

Where is Ben? Does he realize I am in danger? she asked herself. *Oh my God, does anyone even know I am gone?* Sarah continued to argue within her own thoughts. *Breathe, breathe; just empty your mind.*

Sarah could not empty her mind, so she went back to what she knew about bigfoot. Sarah's thoughts were racing and bouncing off one another. *Calm down and think,* Sarah kept telling herself.

She then recalled a conversation she'd had with a student, Dawn. Dawn had said as a young native girl, she was taught by her mother not to fear bigfoot. They were beings meant to help trapped animals and humans by showing them a safe way out of danger.

Tonight, it was impossible for Sarah not to feel fear. *They were so big. She was so alone. Where was June? She would feel better if she were with June.* She was trying to convince herself to say *one-one-one. Breathe, just say "one" repeatedly.*

None of her strategies subsided her fear and hopelessness. She began to quietly weep again, tears cascading down her face. This tearful waterfall did not stop, even though she kept telling herself to stop. *Breathe and repeat the word "one."*

The older male bigfoot was resting closest to Sarah. He could sense her discomfort and wanted to reach out to this human, as he would any animal in distress. *She must feel so helpless and destitute*, he thought. He felt his duty was to try to calm her. He had brought her to their dwelling; it was his responsibility. Plus, if he calmed her, it would make the situation less stressful for his family. If he could at least soothe her, some of them would get some rest, and maybe the gesture would quiet her fears.

Suddenly, out of the darkness, Sarah saw the big face of the older bigfoot male. She gasped at the sight of his massive body with huge arms and shoulders. Somehow, his seemingly very moist eyes held light. It was a phenomenon that was both amazing and frightening. Quietly, he picked her up, and with one sudden movement, brought her down on the bedding. Putting Sarah between his hairy trunk-like legs and sitting behind her, he wrapped his long arms and legs around her in a basket hold. His head towered over

Sarah, but he seemed to have a noticeably short neck. He tried to encompass her upper body.

The lack of mobility of his neck made the movement awkward. For the size of this creature, his head did not seem that much bigger than hers. She stiffened out of fear but told herself not to struggle. He just kept gently but firmly holding her. There was a smell, but not an overbearing gamey smell. Her physical reaction was not near gagging at this animal-like smell. Her own animals had smelled worse at times. The older bigfoot occasionally rotated his head with a turn of his upper body toward the outer side of the shelter to get a whiff of the pine in the air. He needed to mask the human's sweet smell, which was almost gagging to him.

He continued to hold her, trying to connect with her, letting her know she was safe in his presence. His heart pumped with a slow, compassionate beat, coinciding with his emotions, which were filled with concern for this human. It was a learned skill he had, to keep his heart in a compassionate beat and not to match her frantic beat as he held her close. His much larger heartbeat would eventually work to coordinate with the human's heartbeat.

She felt his slow, consistent heartbeat on her back, while she challenged her thoughts not to let these monsters feel her fear. *Do not fear them, do not fear them*, she repeated to herself over and over. It was working minutely, as Sarah continued the chant in her mind. She began to relax. Without realizing what she was doing, Sarah was fondling the fine hair on the bigfoot's arm. Her motion was like a child self-soothing by caressing a favorite blanket's ribbon.

The bigfoot's coat was thick with fine hair and a light natural oily feel to it. The hair follicles seemed fine but plentiful. Completely straight, longer hairs grew directly out of the other hair. Sarah assumed these were longer gray hairs.

His embrace brought warmth to Sarah's body; Sarah could not sleep if she were cold. She did not know how, maybe it was the warmth of his body or her concussion, but she actually fell asleep.

After several hours of holding the frightened, injured, female human, the older bigfoot male gently laid her body on the pine bed. He gathered she had little ability to produce heat, so he brushed pine needles around her to keep her warm. The poor thing had less hair than a hairless cat.

It was now his turn to complete the night watch for the family and scan for other creatures in danger. Holding the human was uniquely special, yet it was much like holding any other frightened animal. He hoped to create a personal connection that calmed this frightened animal. *What was this female human doing by herself?* She seemed so weak and frail. She also seemed so naive about the environment she was crossing. It made no sense that this human would be traveling alone. Although she was not entirely alone—she had the horse—but she had not listened to her companion. As he stepped into the evening, he took a deep breath of fresh air. His watch was uneventful; all creatures seemed to be tucked away for the immediate storm.

CHAPTER 18

Ben was exhausted when his head hit the pillow. He would find the local news on the hotel television and fall asleep to it. He looked at his phone, no calls from Sarah. He wondered if she was warm and comfortable in her bunk. He smiled as he visualized her sleeping with a hoodie up to keep her back and ears warm.

The sounds of a rainstorm awoke Sarah. She was alone on her mat. She was still alive and unharmed. Not raped nor eaten, she was grateful for that. *It's sure to come,* she thought.

The rain seemed to continue for hours, at least a day or more. It was not a light rain, but a thunderstorm at first— with all the elements of thunder, lightning, rain, and wind.

When the wind blew hard, very little rain came into the dwelling from the side, and none leaked through the dwelling's dome-like roof. It was an amazing structure. *How were these trees woven like this? The strength and skill it must have taken.* She worried about June: *Is she being protected from the storm? Is she alive? Is she close by?* Her fear of June's demise was enough to bring Sarah to her knees. This time, the tears of love for her horse quietly rolled down her cheeks.

Several bigfoots looked up and took notice of her love and sadness displayed. As she watched the bigfoot family, they seemed to enjoy the coziness of their shelter while they waited out the storm. They gestured to the children with the sounds of the storm. She kept hearing the family make rain-like noises. It reminded her of a story Ben had told her about his daughter, Isabel. He was trying to teach her not to fear the storm, so he took her to the back door to watch a thunderstorm roll across the farmyard. A crack of lightning struck the ground right in front of them. He said the hair on his neck rose, but he stood still, trying to show her daughter everything was okay.

Maybe the bigfoot family had a better handle on teaching their children about storms. They stayed inside, except for an adult occasionally leaving, then returning with a definitively greater wet-animal smell. After the worst of the storm past, the younger bigfoots would leave and return with adult companions. With a quick shake, they seemed almost dry.

The bigfoot family looked so natural in this storm. Sarah was unaware, but while she had been sleeping, they had prepared for the storm. They needed no weather station to tell them the storm was coming. They knew instinctively. They had gathered food and water.

The adolescent and male bigfoots had found a safe place for June under a slight cliff hanging, surrounded by a thick wooded area where she would have shelter, water, and foliage as long as the storm lasted. They enjoyed this horse; she had responded well to their communication. They wanted no harm to come to her when she was under their care. The mare had lost all fear immediately after their initial encounter, which made them enjoy interacting with her. She was intelligent, strong, and playful.

After the rain, the bigfoot family started to move about, leaving the dwelling more often. Eventually, Sarah saw no one around. *Don't they know I could run? If I were to run, is there a trap waiting for me?* Sarah wondered, as she felt caged without bars.

To her delight, interrupting her thoughts, she heard June whinnying victoriously. *She is alive.* Sarah felt a relief, thus creating hope. Even with this hope of survival, she thanked God she had not convinced her family to join her. She would have felt responsible for their safety.

Do I dare move? she considered. *Yes, I must.* She got up, sore. Her head hurt, but nothing appeared to be extremely injured. She easily and quietly walked over the dirt floor through the middle of the dwelling. It was the size of a big room, maybe 20 by 20 according to her estimate, but its circumference was not straight or perfectly round. The walls moved slightly in and out with the base of the trees.

Sarah did not take a long time to analyze the dwelling. This was her time to escape. The entrance was an opening between two trees. She assumed it faced southeast, as the rays of early light coming from the immediate horizon met her while she walked out of the dwelling.

After leaving the dwelling, Sarah followed the sound of June, which led her through a clump of cedar and moss. Her feet were getting wet. Sarah could run away at this point, but she needed to see June. Her concern kept Sarah moving towards the sound.

Sarah came to the end of the cedar grove and entered an open meadow about five times bigger than her round pen at home. It was a nature-made arena with a few scattered maple and aspen trees growing in the opening.

The adolescent bigfoot, who stood taller and more muscular than Sarah, was riding June in the clearing. He was a medium brown color with silky looking hair on his body, arms, and legs. His hand rested on June's shoulder as he rode.

His hands appeared blocky but similar to those of humans. His hefty legs hung along June's side. He had no halter or saddle on her. He was trick riding. The male would run beside her and jump up on her back, riding for several lopes, then tumbling off the other side. June would pace herself with the adolescent and turn around to reunite with him. When the male was mounted on June, he used his legs and a touch of his hands to move June right or left.

Sarah had so often been reminded by Jazabel to do the exact same thing.

He also used his body to slow June down by leaning backwards—or ask her to move faster by moving his body forwards. Occasionally, he would make sounds.

How does he know this? Sarah wondered. *It is as if he took lessons. What a ridiculous thought that is.*

The ease of movement gave the impression that both of them were having a blast of a time. The bigfoot adolescent continued to perform, as confidence exploded from both creatures.

He then looked up towards the top of the hill. Sarah followed his glance. It took her more than a moment, but there on the top of the landscape, the adult male was sitting and watching, possibly observing his own son riding the horse. She never would have noticed on her own the dominant male in the shadows of the tree. He looked too similar to the moss growing on the tree. But there he was scanning the area for any potential danger towards his family or any creature in need of assistance; meanwhile, he enjoyed watching his son's skill and pleasure of riding the horse. He knew how his son longed to have a horse as part of their family; but a horse would slow them down at times. More importantly, possessing an animal was against their natural law.

She did seem to be an exceptional mare for agility and ability, he observed. The dominant male kept a more diligent watch during this morning break of day. He felt he needed to be cautious. The remoteness of their location and the recent storm provided only a thin blanket of safety.

Suddenly June noticed Sarah standing there. Sarah lowered her head, allowing June with the bigfoot on her back to come to her. She patted June for a moment, then reached into her pocket, discovering an apple piece to give June. *What a good girl!*

Sarah wanted to jump on her and ride away. June did not have a halter on, nor could Sarah just jump on her back. Plus, the adolescent bigfoot was already mounted on June. He watched June and Sarah's interaction. He could sense the closeness they had towards each other. Sarah was too sad and afraid to enjoy their moment together. She was so sorry for her part of the events that led them into this danger. Sarah started weeping again.

How can we get out of here alive? Where is this wilderness prison? Sarah looked around, hoping to find something familiar. She noticed the landscape. She observed lupine stems, which had bloomed earlier in the season. Lupine grew slightly further east than where June and Sarah had started their trail ride. The pine and ferns appeared more intense, and there was far more surface moisture. *They must have traveled after I passed out*, she reasoned.

Sarah looked up at the rider and realized the adolescent was quietly waiting for a response from her. His somewhat flat face with a broad nose displayed that he was patiently waiting, not wanting to cause a severe reaction from the human. He was remembering his parental warning about the unpredictable behavior.

Sarah did not want to take too much time away from the young male and the horse, thinking there may be a repercussion. With regret, she pulsed her hands toward June's shoulders and clucked, moving June away from her. Sarah wanted nothing more than to be with June—to jump on her horse's back and ride back to her family. But Sarah did not know where her family was.

As June moved away, Sarah wondered if Jazabel had connected with the trail coordinator. *Does anyone know we are missing?* she asked herself.

Sadly, Sarah watched June trot off with the young male bigfoot on her back. Sarah heard the male cluck, pushing June into a lope. Sarah realized at that point this family of bigfoots had their own communication with themselves and other creatures in nature. Their communication was somewhat like what she had with the horses, but more developed.

It was amazing how the young male and June responded to each other in the open area. After a time, the dominant male bigfoot on the ridge clapped his hands, then made a circular motion, ending the rotation of movement at the location where Sarah was standing. The young male clapped his hands twice, followed by a one clap response from the dominant male.

June was brought back to Sarah. There was no opposition to the dominant male's request to return her horse—no hesitation to the directive. Nothing like, "Come on, Dad. Just one more time!" It was just done.

So obedient, Sarah thought. She looked back up at the ridge, but the male figure had disappeared. In the moment's silence, the dominant male figure appeared out of nowhere next to her. *How could he move from the ridge to where I am standing so quickly?* Sarah struggled to comprehend the mysteries of these creatures.

In the morning light, Sarah got a true feeling of his magnificence. He appeared to be closer to 9 feet tall than the 8 feet that she had thought earlier. He had wide shoulders and long arms. His face was broad with a rather flat nose. There was a slight cone shape at the top of his head, but nothing extreme. And those dark, dark eyes, she felt could read her emotions. She wondered if he knew the sadness she felt—and the amazement and fear that he evoked. His action provoked no fear, only the mere size and unfamiliarity of his being did so.

His hair covered most of his body, but his manhood created a sizable bump under his hair in that area. Sarah was careful not to gawk; that would be impolite.

The bigfoot adolescent stood next to June, now close to Sarah. Sarah knew she would have obeyed the adult male directives immediately out of fear, but she did not sense fear in the adolescent. More respect and admiration, maybe even love. *Are these creatures capable of human emotions? Are emotions owned by humans?* Sarah started to believe that everything they did was based on obedience, respect, and survival within their family unit—not unlike a horse within its herd.

Horses were prey animals; everything they naturally did was for survival. Allowing the adolescent to ride the horse was for pleasure—but done with caution, followed by extreme surveillance. Actions requested by the male or female superiors were followed without hesitation, because hesitation may bring danger.

One of the strongest components of this communication was the way it enabled connectedness. Immediately after the adult male appeared, he made eye contact with his son and touched him, forehead to forehead.

After standing before Sarah, the two males took June into the cedar swamp area. The larger male put his arm around the younger male as they walked away.

Sarah watched sadly, almost doubtful to what she was observing as June disappeared into the woods with the two bigfoots. Fear for June erupted, and tears flowed down her face again. Sarah just stood there. This was her chance to run, *but what about June?*

The female bigfoot with the two younger members approached Sarah. Their movement was silent. For big creatures, Sarah thought the group was very graceful.

The female bigfoot sensed Sarah's sadness and fear. She wondered why the human did not just leave. She could travel slowly. The female had seen more injured animals leave and survive.

The mother informed her children to move slowly and quietly. They escorted Sarah to a fallen log. They had seen humans do this from afar and hoped she would relieve herself.

Sarah was clueless over what they wanted her to do. The little ones sat on the log with their butts hanging over. Then, after some deliberation by the mother, the young female child bigfoot balanced herself on the log and went to the bathroom. After which she promptly covered her waste. An ah-ha moment, Sarah really needed to relieve herself too, so she took the opportunity.

This seemed to disgust the two little bigfoots, as they ran to their mother and clung to her legs. Everything about humans seemed to be unclean. Even the smell of the humans' waste was disguising. *What did they eat?*

The poor human creatures knew nothing about self or ecological preservation. The female went over and covered up the waste with dirt.

Sarah walked back to the dwelling. The group walked with her, as if they were walking with a new neighbor. There was nothing to restrain Sarah except her own fear.

Still not trusting the irrational behavior of the human, the female bigfoot kept herself between her children and the human. The short walk in the morning light gave her a chance to obverse the human. She assessed Sarah's consequences from the fall off the horse by her movement as the human walked. The human seemed to be carrying herself without pain. She was walking slowly, which was appropriate for the head injury, but she showed no sign of imbalance or pain. The female noticed the human's skin was thin, almost iridescent. Her skin was aging but not extremely wrinkled.

The human's eyes were the color of the sky before a snowstorm, a grey blue. The bigfoot found her eyes to be a unique feature and saw her as beautiful, like all creatures.

They walked simultaneously, giving Sarah a chance to observe bigfoot in the morning light at close proximity. There was a mysterious beauty to them, especially the adult female. It seemed as if the darkness of her skin was deeper than its thickness—as if the skin had more than one dimension. Sarah wondered if that was how the bigfoots disappeared into the shadows. The female bigfoot's skin had ridges but a soft leathery look, which was comparable to the appearance of a pair of very expensive gloves. Sarah wanted to touch it but was afraid to do so.

The children looked like their mother, with lighter brown hair and dark black eyes. In their eyes were pools of moisture that gave an endearing innocence and poise. They were not gorilla-like creatures; they were human-like beings, but far more elegant. The children ran and played, moving in and out from the foliage around them, but they never crossed over their mother's stride to Sarah's side.

They moved with the grace of June, with plentiful tumbling. The grace reminded Sarah of the times she would call the horses in and watch as June walked into the feedlot.

Her movement was more graceful than the other horses. She softly placed each hoof on the ground, almost pointing it like a dancer.

The adult bigfoots seemed to glide, somewhat like cross country skiers. Once in a while, the male child would climb up a small pine and hide. The young female would look and look. When she spotted him, she clapped once, he returned two claps, and then she clapped once more. Soon after, the young male would be walking with the group again.

Sarah became mesmerized with the female bigfoot and her children, staring at their hair, their hands, and their eyes. Sarah's thoughts were interrupted with a nudge by the female bigfoot, breaking her trance into a reality of fear. Sarah was startled and looked into the female's eyes. The female bigfoot diverted her gaze down, and Sarah followed the eye movement. There in Sarah's path was an exposed root that would have tripped the unaware Sarah. Sarah sidestepped and automatically said, "Thank you." The female bigfoot pleasingly nodded to her, while thinking *this poor thing has so much to learn to be self-sufficient in nature*. A simple walk was dangerous to her.

CHAPTER 19

Returning to the dwelling, Sarah sat down on her bedding. She was ready to rest for a while. Although she felt physically stronger, she was weak, and her head pounded slightly.

Maybe after I rest, I can come up with an escape plan, she figured, although it seemed as if no one was truly holding her hostage.

The families continually were in the shadows, watching not for the purpose of keeping Sarah prisoner, but out of curiosity and for their own safety.

Later while she was resting, everyone had left the dwelling, leaving Sarah alone. The family returned with a bowl made of leaves and twigs, and full of acorns. Sarah watched the family prepared their meal. A flat stone was placed on the floor, then many acorns were positioned on the stone. The dominant male had another thicker stone, which was held over the acorns, about a foot high. The stone was dropped. When the thicker stone was lifted, the acorns appeared cracked and opened. The father and mother worked together with the male maneuvering the stone. The two younger bigfoots squealed with delight upon the appearance of the cracked acorns. The female bigfoot sorted out the nuts and placed them in a second bowl of water to be soaked. She did so by scooping instead of picking up between her thumb and pointer finger.

The cracking and placing of acorns happened many times. The nuts soaked for some time. The adolescent took out the empty bowl that had contained the acorns and brought it back with more water. The nuts were scooped out of the first bowl and placed into the fresh water.

While the acorns soaked in the bowl of fresh water, the female bigfoot started busying herself with another project. She knew the extracted water removed the bitterness from the nuts and additionally acted as an astringent and disinfectant for skin.

When the family had been out collecting acorns, the female had been gathering tufts of animal fur and plant fluff to make a sponge-like ball. The male bigfoot was proud of his mate's medicinal knowledge of plants and her ability to apply this knowledge, which was mostly innate except some that was taught to her by her mother and grandmother. Grandmother had taught this female bigfoot to be particular in choosing the plant fluff. The fluff needed to be clean and absorbent.

After she gathered the amount of fluff needed, she rinsed it in the lake and let the sun dry out the bacteria. She hoped her actions would make the human stronger so the visit could soon end. She did not mind the human's visit, but the stay was endangering her family. Soon, many humans would be in their area looking for this human.

While outside gathering supplies, the dominant male watched his mate conduct herself, and her deliberate actions stirred a need to enjoy her. He left the acorn picking for a while and went over to his mate. The male helped her pick animal fuzz and plant fluff, but the material did not match her quality control. Finally, they laughed at his inability to assist with this seemingly simple task. The male bigfoot gave the female a gleeful hug and twirled her around, then returned to the grandfather and younger bigfoot to continue with the gathering of acorns.

All the preparation work was completed. Now the female bigfoot would have to approach the human and try to communicate enough to get her to rinse her face and wound with the acorn water. The female brought the bowl and homemade sponge to the human. The bigfoot female sat on the bedding once again. Instead of using the backpack for a barrier between the two of them, she used the bowl. She sensed the human's fear and wanted to approach passively. The female bigfoot put the sponge in the solution, then dabbed the sponge on her own face. Then she offered the sponge to the human.

While Sarah watched the family soaking the acorns, she realized they were making tannin. Because Sarah knew about the tannin from acorns and its properties, she picked up quickly on the directives the bigfoot female wanted her to follow. Sarah wondered how this creature knew so much about the acorns and cleaning process. She was using this ball of organic matter to clean Sarah's face. *How clever*, Sarah thought as she dabbed her face and arms, then gave the sponge back to her captor. The female bigfoot gestured for Sarah to apply the solution to her head wound. Sarah took the ball of tannin solution back and rinsed off her wound. *This is more amazing; how does this bigfoot know the medicinal value of tannin?* The female bigfoot left the human to her thoughts after the task was completed. She was pleased with how uneventful the procedure had been. Maybe the human was more teachable than the female bigfoot had first thought.

Something about the bigfoots' preparation of food reminded Sarah of her son, Levi. Maybe it was the excitement of the little ones. Maybe it was the adults using their environment for tools. Her son, Dylan, knew what tool to use for what job to effectively get it done, but Levi was good at improvising.

The activity reminded Sarah of a time when Levi 's cat, Boba, was missing. Boba was a hunter and could be gone for a few hours. He generally returned with a headless critter. There were times he returned to the porch and settled down on the front steps to be the neighborhood watch cat. On one particular day, Boba did not return. The neighborhood had been in disarray with street construction. Many theories were developed by Levi's friends about Boba's disappearance, including: the construction work caused him to hunt farther out, or Boba happened to jump into a construction worker's vehicle and was relocated.

Levi continued to dismiss the theories and walked the neighborhood, whistling his Boba's special call. After two days of cruising the neighborhood, Levi thought he heard Boba's meow but could not pinpoint the location. That evening, Levi borrowed a predator sound amplifier, which magnified the noise. Generally, hunters would use this device to locate their wounded prey. Levi walked the same area he had previously heard Boba's meow. This time with the aid of the amplifier, Levi followed the sound and found Boba locked in a garage.

After trying to contact the property's owner, Levi jumped the fence and broke Boba out of the garage. Arriving home, Boba drank water until his thirst was quenched. He scolded Sarah continuously with 15 minutes of meowing. *Why didn't she go out looking for him?* he seemed to ask. Maybe he was telling her the details of his captivity.

Sarah could only hope Levi would borrow those amplifiers or come up with a creative plan in finding June and her.

"When I get home," Sarah mumbled to herself, "I'll have my own story to tell you, Boba."

Once again, Sarah did not know if it was the stress or bump on her head, but she was feeling very tired. She was fighting the need to fall asleep but lost the fight. She lay back on her bed of pine and slept. How long, she did not know, but when she awoke, the two little ones were very close to her face.

CHAPTER 20

After eating, the two young bigfoots were given permission to look at the human. They had been very curious. Their parents preferred them to learn under their supervision.

Both the male and female child were almost nose to nose with the human, watching her sleep. They were more interested in this female human than in the mare, unlike their older sibling. Suddenly, the young male tapped Sarah's forehead—probably to determine if it was as hard as his or at least similar. The tap was not meant to hurt, but it was powerful and piercing.

Sarah twisted her face into an expression of pain, put her hand to her forehead, and cried out, "Ouch," while sitting up. Immediately, both young bigfoots looked at each other. They ran to the middle of the dwelling, at first afraid, then amused. The two began mimicking the same gesture of pain and making similar sounds like "ooh" from the backs of their throats. They started laughing and rolling on the floor. They stopped, looking at each other. They did it again, and once again started laughing. Their laughter was more like a young owl hooting rapidly.

The mother bigfoot had a slight smirk on her face, then after a few minutes of the rascally rendition of the human, the mother swung open her arms, cupping her hands, bringing her hand close together but never clapping. The young ones instantly looked at her and sat quietly. Mom's action was as if she wanted immediate quiet without creating any other noise to command the silence. She postured as if she contained all the surrounding sound within her palms. She nodded her head to thank the young ones for their obedience but did not release them from the silence.

After the pain from the tapping subsided, Sarah started to become more curious and somewhat less fearful. She realized the young bigfoots were humorous, which required intelligence. Sarah was in awe of the obedience of the children. Their connectedness with communication was amazing. Less verbal, more movement and gestures, everyone needed to be in tune with the rest.

Think again. Think. What do you remember about bigfoot stories? Sarah kept repeating to herself. She was trying to recall anything she knew about bigfoot—shared with her in literature or a more spiritual context. *Maybe any knowledge I can remember would get me home,* she thought.

She was trying to recall anything about their communication style. She had heard about mysterious tree breaking, clapping, and bird sounds. The communication of this family was more advanced than most humans would have believed—if they believed in bigfoot at all. Sarah realized she was in a unique situation that few humans had experienced. Up to this point in her stay, bigfoot had done nothing to harm her nor June. Actually, they had shown hospitality.

Sarah remembered conversations with her Native American worker and friend at school. What had Karla said? She had looked so serious when she asked Sarah, "They are real, you know?" speaking of bigfoot. "They are here to teach us humility."

Humility, Sarah thought. *Humility is good. It's not scary.*

But then Sarah remembered stories about humans consumed by bigfoots, and about women kidnapped for bigfoot wives. *Oh my god, is that possible? That would be painful. They are huge. Their half bigfoot babies would rip a woman apart!* She remembered a crazy story about a Russian man that bred a bigfoot female.

Wait, wait. Stop this crazy thinking. Karla said more. Sarah needed to think clearly. Karla had mentioned when they appeared before you, change was coming.

Change, what kind of change? Am I about to experience a change in my life?

They were the keepers of nature. The bigfoots kept creatures on a safe path. Had Sarah and June been on an unsafe path?

CHAPTER 21

On the second day of the trail ride, Jazabel tried to call Sarah early in the morning, thinking she could catch her before they resumed for the day. Sarah did not answer. Sarah had warned Jazabel that her phone would probably die with no electricity at the bunkhouse, plus the riders were not to talk or text on the trail.

Jazabel would try calling after lessons that night. She was anxious to get Sarah's details of the ride. Jazabel wanted to see how her prized student, June, handled the trail.

After the day's lessons, Jazabel was still unable to reach Sarah. Jazabel looked through her email history and found the coordinator, Henry Amnes's, number. Jazabel dialed.

"I'm sorry to say it, but I don't have any record of the rider and horse that you are inquiring about," Henry told Jazabel. Jazabel knew Sarah had had problems with using the credit card for payment. She learned from Henry, the coordinator, if the payment was not received, the information about the rider was not recorded by the system.

The phone connection was bad, but what she thought she heard him say was, "A storm moved in, so the trail ride was shortened. There is one horse trailer left in the parking lot. I noticed it had an out-of-state license plate, but that's all I know."

"Okay, thank you," Jazabel offered.

"Call me when you locate the riding team or if you need my help," he added. "You know, some of the off-trail terrain is dangerous. I know the area well enough, so let me know if I can help."

"Thank you," Jazabel answered. "I will keep you posted."

After hanging up, Jazabel started looking for Ben's number. She needed to call him to see if he knew anything about "the hippie lady." *Sarah may not know it, but she means a lot to me,* Jazabel thought.

Jazabel knew she had Ben's phone number somewhere. As she was digging through her drawer of paperwork to look for the number, Ben's call came in. Luckily, Sarah had made sure that Ben had Jazabel's number.

"Have you heard from Sarah?" Ben asked.

"I have tried to call her several times, but I haven't been able to reach her," replied Jazabel.

Ben tried not to be alarming but said, "A few minutes ago, the local highway patrol called me, because they identified my pickup abandoned in a Minnesota park's parking lot. You haven't heard from Sarah since she started the ride?" He was hoping Sarah was just punishing him for taking off on the airplane ride.

Jazabel reported to Ben what she had learned from the trail ride coordinator: "They have no record of Sarah and June. And no, the only message I got from Sarah was a text that she sent you, too."

"Okay, I'm in the air but will touch down at home in about four hours," Ben replied. The storm was slowing him down; he was flying in behind the storm. But landing and renting a car for the rest of the trip would gain him no time. He needed to remain calm and safe so he could find Sarah.

"I checked the weather. There's a huge rainstorm in the area where Sarah and June are, and they won't start any sort of search for them until the storm is over," Jazabel added to the conversation.

Jazabel told Ben that she would load her trail horse and head out to the trail on her own. That way, she and Henry could search for Sarah and June by horse as soon as the weather cleared, since Henry knew the area so well. If the trail ride had ended and everyone had loaded up and left the area, leaving Ben's truck and trailer, something was wrong. She wanted to get to her as soon as possible.

After thinking about the situation, Ben decided to take his airplane near the trail ride. He contacted Sarah's children, asking them drive to the location of the horse trailer. Ben would try to meet Jazabel at the starting point of the trail ride. *What could have happened to Sarah and June?* was the only thought on his mind.

Levi answered Ben's call with concern. In the 10 years that Sarah and Ben had been together, Ben seldom called Levi. "I'll call Dylan and Stara, and we'll meet you there. We should arrive at the same time as you land. Plus, then we will have a ground vehicle," Levi said, his mind spinning. *What did Mom get into?*

Immediately after receiving the call from his brother, Dylan packed up his car with what he thought would be useful, put on his hiking boots, and left his wife and girls at home. He had a five-hour drive ahead of him. He would call work tomorrow.

Ben's son, Mathew was co-piloting the flight back from Montana, so he decided he would help search for Sarah by air. The safety information at the seminar was valuable, but it tired both he and his dad's brains. And now they had a bumpy flight back. He knew his dad was beat.

The family was putting a plan into action. When they arrived, they would work with the local officers. Mathew would search the area by air with Levi and Dylan. Ben and Stara would join the ground crew. Jazabel would be in the saddle. She had asked Henry, the wilderness ride coordinator, to join them, which he agreed to do.

CHAPTER 22

After the storm and the moment with June, Sarah slept again. She had no idea how many days she had been there. While awake, she noticed that the bigfoot family moved about and rested in the dwelling most of the day. The adult figures left systematically. Sarah was thinking they were checking the perimeter for humans or any kind of danger.

The bigfoot family felt they had a duty to complete. It was about keeping nature, and what was within nature, on a safe course. They watched over their families to keep them safe while they rested, and they watched over nature to keep the other creatures safe and the environment as unscathed as possible while they roamed the terrain.

The adults, including the female, methodically left the room with no pretense of communication—re-entering with a rather un-ceremonial return. One mature member would always stay in the dwelling with the three young ones. A young one with an adult may journey out for a short period of time.

Occasionally when the adults returned, the storytelling began: mimicking animals, some sounding like bird calls and utterances made quickly and repetitively. To Sarah, their speech seemed at times undistinguishable except for its varying pitch, speed, or volume.

The bigfoots would periodically sleep, and when awake, they seemed to entertain themselves. Sarah thought they played hide and seek. The children would vanish into the shadows and sometimes adventure outside. After a small amount of time, one of the bigfoot family members would attempt to find them. Great celebration was demonstrated by a mini dance and forehead-to-forehead touching when a bigfoot's hide-and-seek participant could not be found.

To the bigfoot family, it was not a game; it was training for their mission. They needed to be able to vanish into their environment.

Sarah would have a hard time with this game. She seldom could find the bigfoots in their own shelter. They would win every time. The adolescent hid by her, and she would not have known if not for the smell and her heart racing from fear. Maybe her fear gave him away, but he was found by his mother, as what seemed like the hide and seek game to Sarah continued throughout the day.

Later in the game, the younger male decided to duplicate an attempt at using her brother's hiding spot, but with more perfection. The younger bigfoot took special care in creating a dark space within the pine boughs, quietly moving them a little higher on one side. Then he gently maneuvered Sarah's leg to block vision from the others.

She did not feel fear as much as cooperative partnership with the young male. Nothing had happened to her when the adolescent was in her area, so she felt safer. The young bigfoot treated her not as a living being, but as a part of the dwelling's ecosystem. He hid for a long time, until his father clapped once. The little guy clapped back twice, and the father clapped once again. His young son emerged from his hiding place.

The dominant male picked up his young son, with forehead touching forehead, and spun him in a circle. The rest of the group danced around him: mother with baby in arms, grandfather, older brother, and younger sister. *What a grand display for hide and seek,* Sarah thought.

But for the bigfoot family, their little guy was learning to camouflage himself within his natural environment—a crucial skill for the family's well-being.

CHAPTER 23

Ben was very tired. He thought back to the events of the day when both Sarah and he had left the farm. *Don't beat yourself up about the schedule*, he told himself. *It is what it is, and now I must find Sarah and June.*

He thought about the family and decided that grandchildren would not be told much until they knew more. He only wished they were at least flying in the right state, but it would be several hours before they were in Minnesota.

How many days had it been since anyone had heard from Sarah? Three days, and it would be four before the search party was organized and began in the light. This was not good, Ben thought. *At least it is not bitterly cold out. Sarah hates being cold.* He thought of how she started wearing her cuddle duds before the first snow. Sometimes she would wear three layers of clothes to bed. *What a goof,* Ben had thought. By the time he figured how to get her out the first two layers of clothing, he was too tired to do anything.

Meanwhile, as the dominant male entered the dwelling, Sarah thought, *Oh my gosh, the male shows his love just like Ben shows his love.* His love language was working and providing for his family.

The male bigfoot seemed to need more physical attention from his mate than Ben did. He proudly brought in a great, big armload of shiitake mushrooms. They were in a cotton mesh bag. *Wherever did he find them or the bag? Who knows, but it wasn't the local market,* Sarah laughed to herself.

Shiitake mushrooms did not grow in the wild around Minnesota. That evening, the dominant male had been searching for food rather close to a human's territory— feeling confident, because he had been in this area around the small, quiet river many times.

Near the river, a small home was occupied by a female human. The male bigfoot had seen her many times in the woods. He had traveled the thick forest behind her home to check on the elderly couple that lived deeper in the forest. This female human spent a fair amount of time in the woods while at her home—which was seldom—plus she was very predictable, traveling over the same trails through wooded area every time she explored.

He could keep a watch on her. If they became too close to each other, the bigfoot could simply make an unfamiliar noise or rattle some brush, which was enough to send the female human retreating back to her yard.

On this day of gathering food for his family, he had found a curious mushroom garden. The female human must have designed the growing apparatus. It was a strange vision of an oak log with holes bored into it. The board was soaking in a trough of fresh water. Growing out of the holes were shiitake mushrooms with flat but round heads.

The female would have been delighted to know bigfoot ate some of her mushrooms. She thought she heard them occasionally milling about her property.

His mate would definitely be pleased with his find. The male took enough to feed his family, making sure to leave spores growing for more harvesting. He would never totally rob the female human of her labor. She had done a nice job of producing mushrooms.

As he left, the male chose rocks and fallen logs as steps, while carefully leaving the mushroom garden. He had many years of experience leaving an area undetected.

In leaving he also noticed a gosling in a panic, searching the area around the garden. The confused, downy, young gosling had not followed closely behind his mother. The bigfoot male shooed the little one in the direction of his mother. Tonight, the little one would not be dinner for another animal.

CHAPTER 24

When entering the dwelling, the bigfoot male promptly gave the mushrooms to his mate. Sarah thought she may have seen a smile on both of their faces. *Were they flirting?*

It seemed as if all the family members enjoyed the affection the dominant male and female had towards each other. Their strong bond created a stronger family.

The older male thought fondly about his deceased mate, while the adolescent hoped to find a female as competent and loving as his mother, and the youngest were just empathically happy. The male bigfoot must have been considered handsome. *Whatever that meant?* Looking like he could complete any task asked of him, together with apparent confidence, made anyone attractive.

A scar was carved right above his left eye. It did not take away from his handsomeness, but it added to his fierceness. Sarah thought it weird to observe, but he seemed to be in love with his mate. His eyes softened as he looked into every family member's eyes, but especially hers. She was a smaller bigfoot but looked very muscular and feminine. They each had an egg-shaped head, more pointed on top, but not as extreme as Sarah had seen in drawings. Sarah thought they were a healthy lot of bigfoots; she considered it was a result of caring for each other.

Later that evening after the baby had been nursed and everyone was settled in, the dominant male and female left the dwelling. The male bigfoot knew that having the human and horse nearby had brought stress to his mate. He wanted to have private time with his mate to relax and satisfy her. He found a pastoral spot under a tree, not far from the shelter. He laid her down under the tree. Her beauty only added to the natural beauty of the night. He touched and nibbled where he knew she enjoyed the attention. She felt she was privileged to have him as a lifetime mate. He had been her only mate, and he was an excellent partner in many ways.

After they shared their love, they rested in each other's arms. As they rested, the female wondered about the human. She was aging, *but did she have a life mate? Was someone looking for her?* The human was sweet, never aggressive towards them. She was a fearful little creature, poor thing. After a time, they got up and returned to the dwelling. Their intimacy would be a memory that was part of them forever.

CHAPTER 25

Sarah had been in their dwelling for possibly three days or more. With concussion-induced sleep and the time of the storm, it was hard to determine exactly how long.

The bigfoot family had done nothing to feed her embodying fear. They had dressed her wounds, offered her food, taken care of her horse, and given her a place in their home to recover from her injury. Although she was not completely convinced of their good intentions, her fear was losing force over her thoughts.

She watched as they went about their day. Occasionally, they would try to reach out to her by offering her food or water—or taking her out to "the log."

Sarah noticed the family forming a circle on the floor, alternating child and adult. The dominant male began the activity by creating a blue jay sound, proceeded by nodding at each family member, one at a time. The young male child sitting next to his dad created the same sound and nodded to everyone around the circle. When the child completed the circle, the mother took her turn. She made the wonderful blue jay sound, then nodded to everyone. It was the baby's turn. The baby's sound was much like a beeping coo.

They appeared to be a team as the mother looked into her baby's face and repeated the bird sound several times, then the baby tried nodding to everyone. Sitting next to the mom was the young female. Being younger than her brother, she repeated the bird call of *hello* with some difficulty. Delighted at her attempt, she nodded to all the members.

Everyone had a turn. It was somewhat like the human game of telephone, but Sarah analyzed it as a game that taught the sounds and familiarized the family members with each enunciation.

It was the young male's turn to start the repetition. He made the sound of a robin in distress, then looked around as if to check his environment for danger. Now it was the mom's turn to mimic the sound and act out its meaning. The baby gave it a try and did a much better job of this sound. Apparently checking the environment was a new concept to her, as her eyes and head bobbed about.

Sarah thought, *So adorable, and so much encouragement from all.* Next the young female child did an excellent robin sound and overacted the gesture of observation.

It was grandfather's turn. Before he made his communicative sound, he stood up and walked over to Sarah. He took her hand, which was much smaller than his, and led her to the circle. She sat between the grandfather and adolescent. Grandfather made the robin call, then visually searched the area for danger. After he had completed his turn, he turned to Sarah and nodded his head to move her into her turn.

Sarah figured it out and turned to make the robin sound, then scanned the dwelling with her eyes. Her sound made the group chuckle very slightly, but it was accepted. The group seemed to use only positive reinforcement.

After the circle of bigfoots completed their turn on the robin call, it was Sarah's turn to lead. She thought about how to communicate via the bigfoots' method. She remembered the father had made a bluebird tweet for "hello." Sarah said, "Hello," then she made a sincere attempt to make the bluebird tweet. Sarah then nodded a hello to everyone in the circle.

She turned to the adolescent bigfoot for his turn to repeat her communication. He made more of a meow sound. Creating the hello sound, as he filled the back and top of his mouth, created a bass echoing in his mouth. The adolescent tweeted and nodded an acknowledgement to everyone in the circle.

It was the father's turn next. He was able to mimic the "h" sound, getting closer to the word "hello." Then he gave a quick tweet and nodded to the other members. It felt strange to him to say a human word, but it could be helpful to address a human in their native language, even with only one word.

After everyone gave it an authentic try, it seemed as if they giggled with satisfaction at the hard task they had all attempted.

After Sarah's turn, the adolescent made a "caw" like a crow and pointed to Sarah. Then they went around the circle doing the same sound and pointing at Sarah. When it was Sarah's turn, she knew it meant human. So, she cawed, pointed to herself, and said "human." The family responded back with trying to say human in unison.

Later that day, Sarah wondered if "caw, caw" would mean two humans. Sarah was rethinking the sound concept. *Were they actually forming words and teaching the little ones their words?* She remembered hearing similar sounds of tongue clicking and whistles when she had listened to a Lakota speaker. It was very rhythmic.

At dusk that night, it was lovely out. The air was still, and the temperature hovered around 70 degrees. The female bigfoot walked over to where Sarah was sitting on her mat. She held Sarah's chin and gently turned Sarah's head, tenderly touching Sarah's head injury. They were so close, Sarah could see the texture of the bigfoot's skin. Sarah thought the female was taking notice of her skin unilaterally. With Sarah's check-up, she noticed the smell of a bigfoot was becoming somewhat acceptable to Sarah, as hers apparently was becoming acceptable to the bigfoot family. They seemed not to have to politely hold their breath anymore.

Sarah considered this encounter as one of her nurse check-ups, except she was not asked to roll up her sleeve. After completing the check-up, the female bigfoot walked to the adolescent male and communicated something to him.

The female selected a dry plant she had hanging in their dwelling amongst other plants. She grabbed the plant and moved directly to Sarah. The female then picked up Sarah's pack and took Sarah by the hand. She began leading her out of the dwelling and down to the lake area. The female bigfoot indicated to Sarah she should take off her clothes by pulling lightly upward on Sarah's T-shirt. Sarah took off her shirt and pants but left her gross, crusting bra and panties on. Sarah would never expose herself in public, let alone to a bigfoot.

The female bigfoot did not bother with trying to get this human totally naked. She simply took her hand again and walked her into the sandy, hard bottom of the lake.

The female bigfoot was careful not to trigger the human's fear. Instead, she slowly attempted everything she needed the human to complete. After they were knee deep in the lake, the female lightly splashed water over Sarah. The female began to wash herself. Sarah watched for a moment, then Sarah mimicked the female bigfoot's actions. Eventually, the female bigfoot leaned back and wet her hair with clean lake water exactly where Sarah's injury occurred on her head. She followed that action with going under the water. Sarah did the same thing.

She finally realized the female wanted her to wash her wound.

After Sarah was clean but still in the water, the adolescent brought June into the water. The female had earlier arranged the timing of bringing the horse into the water with the human. She knew Sarah would enjoy it. In fact, Sarah had always dreamed of experiencing the joy of playing in the water with her horse.

Sarah smiled at June's reaction to the lake. At first, June pawed at the water, making huge splashes. She drank the water and gingerly walked deeper into the lake. June enjoyed the water. Both the adolescent bigfoot and Sarah were laughing.

June noticed Sarah in the water and walked over to her. "Sorry, sweetie. No treats in my pockets, because I have no pockets," Sarah told her. But June did not care. She wanted to be near Sarah.

Sarah was not much of a swimmer, but the water was shallow and perfectly safe. With the buoyancy of the water, Sarah was able to mount June and ride bareback—without a halter. *Simply amazing*, she thought. They were in the water until it got quite dark.

Sarah had noticed the female bigfoot was on the shore, mixing the crumbled, dry plant; dirt; and water together. The adolescent came with a vine-like rope and put it around June's neck. He led June with Sarah on her back over to his mom. He helped Sarah slide off June. *Truly a young gentleman*. He took the horse away.

The female handed Sarah her pack. Sarah was happy to remember she had a light, micro-cloth towel and change of clothes in the backpack.

At this point, Sarah changed everything from underwear to pants. The female walked up to Sarah, cautiously grabbed the hair around the wound, and moved it out of the way as much as she could while applying the mud pack. The female kept saying the same three sounds over and over, communicating that she was dressing her wound, which was almost completely healed.

As the female moved the hair away from the bump, she wondered what the human's fine hair was good for anyway, besides being very pleasant to touch. It did not keep one warm, nor was it attractive. Its positive quality was soft fineness.

Sarah took a moment to comb out the hair as best as she could, so as not to disturb the wound. It occurred again to Sarah that this bigfoot family was actually looking after her well-being.

While Sarah was primping, she reached into her pack, brought out a container, and applied bug spray. Sarah thought she noticed a slight distaste on the female's face when she applied her chemicals. After Sarah was done with dressing, she nodded her head and caught the bigfoot female's eyes for a thank you. The female's almost black, beautiful eyes softened, as she nodded back to Sarah.

Sarah pleased the female by beginning to communicate without the extreme fear. Sarah took a moment to wash out her dirty laundry before returning to the shelter. She would hang her garments on a branch to dry. She did not know how long she would be there, so keeping a clean set of clothing would be beneficial.

While Sarah was washing her things, she saw the female give a hollow-like clap with cupped hands, and in return heard the bigfoot grandfather and the two little ones clap back twice. Then the mother responded with a clap.

So much for humans developing the kindergarten phrase "clap once if you hear my voice," Sarah thought.

As she sat on the shore of the lake, a big rock splashed into the water. It did not hit close enough to hurt anyone, but it created a large splash. The younger male picked up the largest rock he could muster and threw it back at the splash. It was amazing how much strength the little guy had. After the second splash, a deep, gleeful growl was followed by a click that filled the air. He seemed to please his father.

The young female tumbled about with grace and power. The baby clapped. Sarah responded by clapping also. It seemed the younger bigfoot male had his father's talents and strength.

Later that night, everyone was out of the dwelling except the grandfather and Sarah. The older male had noticed Sarah was picking up some of their communication. He thought he would push her into learning more quickly.

The evening was clear, while the moon and stars lit up the sky. The older male led Sarah outside to a grassy area where she could see the horse. He hoped that would calm her, and she would learn easier without fear. He did have a concern that the human would focus too much on the horse, but he would give the lesson a try.

Sarah's attention went to the family gathered not far away. The mother bigfoot was cradled from behind by her mate. He was rubbing her neck and slowly running his hands over her arms and leg. The baby was sitting in its mother's lap. And the two toddlers were hanging on Dad's back, taking turns jumping on and tumbling off. They would rush their older brother, who was sitting several yards away, then rush back to Dad.

What a delightful display of affection to watch.

Finally, the grandfather started with the caw and pointed to Sarah. This snagged Sarah's attention. Then he twisted his finger into his palm and made a wrenching face, while making a new sound that Sarah had never really heard before in human language. Moving the fingers while he had twisted his voice, he touched the back of his head. The human had hurt the back of her head. Sarah nodded and repeated the communication of sound, *cay-ye*, back to the elder bigfoot. It impressed the bigfoot how quickly she picked up the communication.

Then Sarah initiated the communication. She pointed to herself and said "Caw, human," then pointed to the male and opened her hands to question what the bigfoot was called. He pointed to his family and then himself. He took a moment and rubbed his hands together, clapping his thigh and using his mouth to create the sound of rain in a strange way with utterance and movement. After creating this sound, he stopped.

The older male pointed to himself. With his hands and his mouth, he made the sound of one raindrop. It was a word with a tap on his thigh.

Sarah gathered that the family or clan had the name of "rain," but the grandfather's name was that of one raindrop.

Sarah tried desperately to make the sound of one drop.

She remembered having the same difficulty in learning the students' names. It took her several months to get the name "Anahi" right. Sarah would blame her

Norwegian brain for the difficulty. She often wondered if she had a learning disability with recreating sounds correctly.

But in the forest, she did not feel judged by her failed attempts. She accepted that learning to use her mouth and tongue to create a totally different language was difficult.

The bigfoot responded with a nod of pleasure at Sarah's attempts. Sarah pointed at herself and said, "Caw," again, then paused and said, "Sarah."

He twisted his mouth and tried but said, "Sarah."

Sarah pointed at him and tried the raindrop sound again.

They both chuckled.

Then the bigfoot gently took her shoulders and touched his forehead to hers. The tender connection brought tears to her eyes and filled her heart with warmth. It was more than the physical touch; it was as if he sent the emotion and feeling into her heart and mind.

CHAPTER 26

After their language lesson, Sarah went back into the dwelling and sat on the bed, thinking about what she had learned. She noticed the female sitting with the baby and the two younger children in the middle of the dwelling. They were mixing plump, bluish-red, wild berries with the leftover acorn nuts.

Sarah remembered she had packed several apples for her first night ride. She walked over and stood by the small circle of bigfoots, making eye contact with the female and nodding to her. The female nodded back.

Sarah handed the apples to the female. Sarah said, "Thank you," then tried to make the injury sound she had learned and touched her head. Sarah was trying to thank the female bigfoot for taking care of her.

Sarah thought the female bigfoot understood the message as she accepted the apples.

Sarah sat down next to the younger male bigfoot. He looked up to her with no expression. *It is good to see he is not repulsed!* she thought. *He is a husky little guy.* Apparently, he was brave enough not to move away from this human. He accepted his mother's judgement in allowing the human to sit with them.

The female bigfoot had been seriously thinking about the human. She decided the human was not there to hurt them. The human's bond with the mare was sincere. Except for the first attempt to run, the human's behavior was rational. The female bigfoot had no reason to distrust her. She felt no danger from this human—just gratitude and kindness from her.

In a gesture of trust, the female bigfoot reached her baby girl over to Sarah. Sarah was honored to take the little one. The baby looked up at Sarah and reached up to touch her fine, greying, blond hair. The baby fondled it and gave it a yank. Sarah gently loosened the baby's grip.

The bigfoot mother reached out to the baby's hands. The baby released her grip, but not without still holding a few strands of hair.

Sarah took both hands into hers and started clapping the baby's hands. The baby giggled and cooed. She was truly adorable to Sarah. Her deep, round, black eyes and chubby cheeks made her look so healthy. Her hair was slightly wavy but not as long as the adults' locks. It seemed to have the texture and feathering of a golden retriever, but darker in color, very lustrous and functional.

Sarah put her face close to the baby's. Her skin was similar to her mother's, lips were full, nose was slightly flat— but once again, her head was not cone shaped as Sarah had expected of a bigfoot.

As Sarah leaned in, she said, "Baby."

The baby cooed a different sound back. For a moment, Sarah wished she could keep this little one. *What am I thinking? They are not animals. I have no right to think that.* The baby felt safe and moved her forehead toward Sarah's, and they touched.

The baby made the same sound. Not really knowing what this word meant, Sarah was sure it was a word of endearment. Sarah repeated the sound that was close to, "Caw." Sarah gave the baby back to her mother, and the little male moved closer to Sarah. Sarah took the opportunity to teach him patty cake. He was so determined to repeat the pattern, that she was impressed.

While playing patty cake, Sarah noticed he had five fingers, but the little finger was so minute, it was near nonexistent.

After he mastered the game, Sarah taught patty cake to the little female bigfoot. The little female learned quickly. She had been watching her brother and had rehearsed the patterns in her mind. She did make mistakes, but that did not steal her gusto from the game. She continued playing with enthusiasm.

Their mother observed that Sarah's face was full of joy and caring. Sarah had played this game many times with her children and grandchildren. She looked up at the female bigfoot. Her face was soft with love and pride for her children.

After the playing time was over, Sarah stayed in the circle and ate with the group. She nodded a thank you to the female and thought she would take the opportunity to try and communicate with her. Sarah tried to indicate the dominant male first by trying the rain sounds with her mouth and hands.

The female was pleased she had learned their family name.

Not knowing the dominant male's name, she tried to identify him by showing his size with her hands. After she indicated the dominant male, Sarah drew her three fingers above her left eye where the distinguished scars were on his face. Sarah tried desperately to make the injury word the older male had taught her.

The female bigfoot understood exactly what Sarah had asked. She repeated Sarah's gestures, beginning to tell the story. She used the grandfather's name.

Sarah nodded, knowing she meant the older male.

Then she said another word which Sarah didn't understand, a twisted tongue-click with a "shhh" sound after it. Finally, the female pointed to herself.

Sarah understood the female was talking about the grandfather's mate. The story told seemed to suggest the mate and adolescent male had been out picking berries. The female used the berries in front of them with picking actions to communicate. A mother bear had attacked them. Her mate had been keeping watch, but by the time he got to the grandmother, she was dead. The boy was saved.

At times, Sarah did not follow the details, but the female bigfoot told the story with such emotion, Sarah knew the magnitude of the loss felt for the older bigfoot grandmother's death.

The death of the bear was tragic to the family. The bigfoots were not predators like the humans had assumed. Sarah had never seen them eat meat. The bigfoot family may have eaten meat outside of their dwelling, possibly to keep the dwelling clean and free of the smell of decaying flesh, but she had only seen them eat vegetation.

As Sarah's fear subsided and her relationship with the family began to grow, she began to think beyond her own safety. Her presence brought danger to them. They had done nothing to harm June or her. Sarah knew it was time to leave.

How could I do anything to bring harm to these beings? she thought. She felt healthy and strong, resulting from the good care of this bigfoot female.

Holding the female's eye contact, Sarah said, "Caw," pointing at herself. Sarah pointed to her wound and crossed her palms several times—hopefully saying it was healed and gone. After that, Sarah walked her index finger and middle finger of her right hand across her left hand. Sarah pointed to the opening of the dwelling.

The female bigfoot pointed at Sarah, said the sound, "Caw," and repeated the motion. She agreed with Sarah; she was ready for the human visitor to leave. Although the human had been gracious and showed eagerness to learn, the human needed to be with humans. The female bigfoot would relay the message to the males.

Sarah bowed to the bigfoot female and stood up. The female also stood up and walked over to Sarah. With great tenderness, she took Sarah's shoulders and, while keeping eye contact, gently touched her forehead to Sarah's. Sarah leaned into her, feeling an overwhelming compassion.

Sarah walked out of the dwelling, and using her senses, found her way to June. There in the small pasture, the two spent their last time in this Minnesota wilderness area. They felt the cool breeze, listened to the birds, and swatted more than a few bugs. Luckily, a large portion of her body was covered.

She took this time to review her decision. She felt healthy. June look wonderfully athletic as she moved close to Sarah, while she was gently touched by her partner's hand. June felt content being close to the elderly women.

Sarah's mind drifted to the farm and all of her loved ones. *How she missed everything and everyone.*

So often, we stand in a world of conflict. Sarah reflected on the inner conflict of wanting to learn more from her experience with the bigfoot family and wanting desperately to be home.

She said her goodbyes to June for now. June knew something was changing. Sarah put her cheek to June's cheek and went back to the dwelling.

CHAPTER 27

The female bigfoot relayed Sarah's wishes to the other adults. After some deliberation amongst the group, it was determined the two older males would get the human as close as possible to her humans.

The bigfoot travelers needed time to properly move the female and horse out of their area while taking mutual care of their family.

The female bigfoot tried to let the human know the plan by making a half circle over her palm while looking up at the sky, which Sarah interpreted to mean this would happen the next 12 hours.

There was a feeling of sadness knowing she had to leave. All her fear had left her, and every moment she was awake she was learning from these wonderful creatures. She was learning their communication methods, but more importantly, she felt their connectedness to each other and to nature—something Sarah did not always feel with people.

Here, everything and everyone has value, Sarah reflected. *Back in my world, everyone is so busy; money, work, and time has its value, but this connection which feels so real here doesn't always feel real in my world. As my fear subsides, I feel like I can understand their intentions.*

As Sarah was thinking about preparing to leave, the dominant male entered the dwelling with something on his mind. He did not enter with his usual contentment or with food for the group. This time, he had some knowledge that he was communicating to the rest of the adults. There was something going on out there—humans—and somehow Sarah was involved.

Was there a search party? She had been gone with no communication for several days. Sarah did not know what was going on within the bigfoot group. The family was concerned about what to do with the human and the horse—how to travel close enough to the search party to keep the human safe but far enough to keep themselves safe.

They had a mission to follow to the end. The adolescent was given the opportunity to take part in the decision making. Of course, he wanted to keep June. That was out of the question. The older male was explaining with gestures and utterance, "But son, there are more important details to attend to right now," he seemed to be saying.

The male turned his attention to address these details with everyone. The grandfather believed this female human would not cause them harm by supplying the other humans with their location, nor did she even know where she was. But the dominant male did not know how they could guarantee her silence about their existence.

Since the beginning of time, when bigfoots assisted an animal throughout the wilderness, the creatures generally assumed they were being assisted. Plus, they had no reasonable way to endanger the bigfoots' existence. This time, with the human being injured and having a horse, they were accountable for the safety of both creatures. In doing so, they had unintentionally shown their guest the daily patterns of the bigfoot family within their own dwelling. This was something they would rather that humans did not know.

The dominant male firmly believed she would never be able to find her way back to the bigfoots on her own. She was not clever enough. Nor did he believe she knew they had saved her and the horse from potential harm. She had not been their captive. They agreed the human thought she was a hostage, although the family had sensed her fear subsiding as she had begun to understand their language and spent more time with them.

Opposingly, the elderly male believed she understood enough of their communication that he could make sure she would secure everyone's survival. He profoundly believed she was understanding their intentions more clearly in the latter time of her stay. He also believed the bigfoots only needed to give the human and her horse a start in the right direction towards the other humans, and she would be found.

He would be willing to do that, if the rest of the adults agreed on the plan.

The dominant male agreed to getting her started in the right direction, if his father could assure the human's alliance.

The second part of their plan would go into play in the darkness of night. The female and adolescent male with the younger children would start moving deeper into the wilderness, into fairly unreachable areas. Their travel would be slower. The two could travel swiftly for many miles, but the younger three would need resting periods.

After dusk, the two older males would take the human and her horse as far as they needed to, and then would turn around to catch up with their bigfoot family. They would be traveling during both night and day, which was not a normal routine of the species.

The female bigfoot would leave markers to assure she was on the planned route. If not, she would leave markers indicating the change, as they had done for years. She could leave in a hurry. There was not much she would need to gather up or pack. They would eat off the land, and she would breastfeed the baby. She knew where caves and established safe shelters were if they needed to stop. Her ability to smell a human a great distance away was well developed. An especially key factor of their existence was their acute senses.

In general, humans were viewed as innately ignorant destructors. Without knowing, they left a path of pain for nature to endure.

CHAPTER 28

Ben and Mathew were met at the small airport near the trail entrance by Levi, Stara, and Dylan. Stara took everyone to the motel less than four miles away from the trail entrance. There at the roadside motel, local agents had set up a center and reserved rooms for the family and search party. There was no real lobby at the motel, so for the search party, one of the sleeping rooms would double as a communication center. Mathew, Levi, and Dylan would return to the airplane in the morning and start the air search.

As the planning began with Jerry, the local sheriff, some conflict arose. Ben had definite opinions on how the rescue should be carried out. He did not want the Civil Air Patrol called.

"I am actually a Lieutenant Major in the Civil Air Patrol, and we are not asking them to search with us," he stated. He believed their regulation on 1,000-foot elevation within a mile grid would be totally fruitless. Plus, Mathew—with Levi and Dylan's eyes—could do an excellent job.

Ben interrupted Jerry and started instructing Mathew. "Fly as closely to the tree line as safety allows," he said. He wanted the three boys to put any known trails into the plane's GPS.

"I sent a ground crew out over the trails yesterday, but none of them left the designated trail," Jerry interjected.

Ben ignored Jerry and kept briefing the young men. "Mathew, I want you to do nothing but fly. Levi and Dylan, watch out the right and left windows." At times, they were to sit on the right side and watch the same area together, he explained. "Look for smoke or anything that would indicate a human being or horse. If at any time you become tired, Mathew, turn around and land. If possible, circle the same area twice, just in case Sarah hears the plane and comes out of the trees into a clearing to be seen."

That is if Sarah is mobile, he thought. Ben worried about her health.

Jerry tried to inform Ben: "There are really not many clearings in the area. We will be searching beyond the trail ride this time out." Jerry had a topographical map of the tornado damage from the previous year. He patiently waited for Ben's aerial instructions to be completed.

Jerry noted that Ben appeared very professional. Jerry would give him the aerial part of the search, but feet on the ground were his responsibility. Plus, Ben was too close to the missing person to put him in charge of everything or try to correct him at this point. Jerry would be the incident commander. They had to follow FEMA regulations. The ground search party would walk slowly. *Hopefully, they would find Sarah before the ravines got too deep or too many fallen trees crossed the path. It would be difficult to get a body and horse out of the area.* These thoughts he kept to himself.

Before leaving the city, Stara had completed organizing a conference. Her company insisted that she take all leftover water bottles and food for the search party. The supplies were already valuable. The people who were not planning the search operation sat quietly listening and eating. Many were too afraid to think about the possibilities. At dawn, it would be five days since Sarah had been seen. It was taking some time to mobilize the search party.

Jazabel joined the planning meeting. She had hauled Hank to the site. Henry was coming with his horse. They would search by horse, while Jerry, Ben, Stara, and local volunteers searched by foot.

Everyone sat for a while in their own thoughts. Ben's mind was busy pondering how to cover the most ground effectively. Dylan was preparing some sight equipment for Levi and himself. Levi was looking at the trail maps while assisting Mathew with the GPS. Stara wondered why her mother couldn't be satisfied with retirement like most women were. *Why couldn't she just travel on cruises?* she thought, her mind wandering. *First, she started rescuing horses, then training horses, and now this trail ride. What happened to saving the children, like most of her life's work?*

Stara had found out the night before that Jazabel had been one of her mom's students. Stara remembered the story of the student taking off on her mom. It had concerned Sarah greatly and been one of the nights when Sarah had to work late, leaving Stara on her own. Her brothers were already out of the house. It was more emotional for Stara than she thought it would be to connect with the elements of her mother's past that had shaped her life.

Jazabel had no clue about this part of Sarah's family members' lives. Jazabel showed no emotion to hint at how dear Sarah was to her. She instead left the meeting to attend to her horse. She had no need to further communicate with the family; it would be too revealing for her. She valued her personal comfort zone. *They are Sarah's family—a family I will never belong to,* she told herself. In her own way, she was part of Sarah's world, which was better than family.

Jazabel wanted to sleep in a makeshift camper in the horse trailer. Henry would arrive with his horse before dawn. It seemed like a good idea to settle in.

Jazabel's departure was a cue for everyone to settle in for a few hours before they set out. In the morning, Stara and Ben would drop the boys off at the airport and head to the parking lot—which would serve as the command location, the main site for all law enforcement, volunteers, and family to meet. Stara had been designated the information liaison—keeping ground, local law enforcement, air, and horse search parties informed on all actions. She was very capable of phone and radio communication. Her organizational skills and no-fuss attitude would come in handy.

CHAPTER 29

The older bigfoot male moved in close to Sarah's face. It was important for the human to understand what they needed from her. The older male did not want harm to come to the female human and her horse by leaving her alone or with just any group of humans, nor did he want to take chances with his family's well-being.

She seemed so vulnerable, and at some level, she had connected with him. The horse had communicated and connected well, especially with his grandson. He would do his best to help her understand that her silence about their existence was crucial to the survival of themselves and nature.

The older male started with direct eye contact with Sarah, then he looked around the dwelling at every family member. He created a movement much like the one the mother had done with the younger ones when she wanted the two to quiet down. This gesture symbolized holding all the noise in the air and containing it in his palms. He repeated it several times by raising his arms in the air, then slowly lowering his cupped hands. He brought them together as if creating a vessel to hold the noise in the dwelling.

The next gesture he made was to bring two of his fingers to the front of his mouth. Then he pinched his mouth shut.

Again, he brought his palms up. Capturing the noise between them, then taking his two fingers, he touched Sarah's lips and pinched them closed.

Sarah understood. She almost heard the words within her head. He was asking her for her silence about their existence. Her eyes revealed she understood. Sarah raised her arms high, cupped her hands, and brought them almost together as if she were catching all the noise. She then touched her lips and pinched them closed. Because she wanted the physical interaction, she did it one more time, but this time she actually touched the elder bigfoot's lip and gently pinched them shut.

The older bigfoot lumbered over and touched his head to her forehead. He held the pose for a moment, then moved away.

Sarah had tears in her eyes, but this time not tears of fear. Sarah had just promised the older male she would not speak of what she had observed. This truly meant their survival.

He was trusting her to follow through. Strangely, she felt she had a friend in him. What Sarah finally realized was the importance of the bigfoots in the nurturing of nature. The bigfoot creatures were the balanced caretakers of nature—with humility and connectedness of everything that existed within nature. They were magnificent creatures that were intelligent, compassionate, and capable. She felt she could do nothing to jeopardize the existence of this family. Their connectedness had touched her in many ways. She had seen a little slice of humanity within their home-like dwelling.

Sarah knew the urgency of swift and precise evacuation. It meant their survival and, if she cooperated, her well-being. And more important to her, it meant preserving June's well-being, too.

Sarah felt well enough to be on the move. While she was excited to see her loved ones, she was sad she would not be able to share her experience with anyone. It was unique and rewarding; she regretted she had wasted time being fearful. *How often in my lifetime have I been too fearful or hesitant to take an opportunity?* she reflected. By nature, she was not anxious, yet she had that negative and fearful thought process that loomed over many humans—the fear of the unknown. *The fear of a different culture, of changing jobs, of moving and meeting other people.* Sarah reflected on the countless fears that drove society.

After the elder bigfoot confirmed that Sarah would be their ally, everything moved quickly. There was no time for rest. The female bigfoot hoped Sarah had the stamina to hold up until she was found by her kind. She lamented to herself, as the human had been a cooperative patient.

Goodbyes were made bigfoot style. The dominant male went to each of his family members, making eye contact with each one. One more time, as she had seen often, he leaned into their foreheads. The baby seemed to giggle with Dad's affection. The moment of intimacy lasted quite a bit longer with the female bigfoot—not merely longer, but deeper. It was obvious he had adoring affection towards her and was concerned about her. He knew that she was given a great responsibility to take their children and move forward. She would travel with the adolescent and other three children until they met at another location. The two male bigfoots would make sure the human and horse got far enough back to be safely found—which meant they would be dangerously close to the other humans.

The male bigfoot needed to move undetected when traveling back through the cedar marsh, so that the humans could not follow their tracks. In their travels towards the drop-off, they would use designated trails developed by humans. Therefore, the human and horse could travel with less difficulty and more speed.

They had done it before, by traveling through campgrounds without the campers knowing. This time with a horse, it would not be as easy. They would not leave the human and mare with any group of campers. They had observed their cruelty before. Even if they were her kind, the bigfoots wanted to get her close to her own humans— people who would care for her and the horse. Hopefully, the larger group of humans would disperse when they found the female human and the horse, making their own retreat less dangerous. They needed to move quickly and cunningly.

As soon as darkness fell over them, the family moved out, separating from the group but planning to reunite as soon as possible. They knew of their established rendezvous locations and would reunite in a more remote location.

Sarah had observed their communication behavior over the last few days. She knew they would use a call-and-response technique. Sometimes they used developed methods of clapping that sounded somewhat like the pounding of hollow trees or knocking of larger sticks together. There was the series of whistles also used in locating each other.

What Sarah did not realize was the bigfoots' level of consideration given to keeping her safe and returning her to the path that would lead her to her human family.

There were no cell phones for the bigfoot family to use for communication once they separated. Until they were closer to their destination, their communication consisted of clues they left for each other, clues left for many generations.

Sarah's eyes adjusted to the vastness as she was led out of the dwelling. She saw June waiting for her. No saddle, but she was haltered with the reins.

Sarah was given her mosquito netting shirt, including a hood that she had packed in her backpack. She was directed to put it on, which she did. The older male gently but firmly grasped Sarah and threw her over his shoulders. This behavior was a new experience for both of them. She did not feel fear; she felt protected and cared for.

He then started running. The dominant male was right behind them, leading June. June did not hesitate. She obediently followed the runners, adjusting her pace to the bigfoots' pace.

It did not take long before their gait changed. The bigfoot males, the human, and the horse moved more slowly than the bigfoots hoped to, but that was understandable. They were covering ground amongst the dampest of the cedar swamp, which pulled them in one step at a time.

They had not wanted the human's weight on the horse. It could cause the mare to be off balance and overworked. Their additional concern was the horse would panic with extra weight on her back in the marsh.

The mare was not used to traveling in the marsh, but they were. This marsh was not large; they could travel the edge, which was somewhat dryer. The older male would adjust easily to the moist ground.

Sarah was amazed at the speed she felt. But being carried like a potato sack did not help her correctly determine the reality of their speed, nor did it help her head. As a slight pounding began, she would not let the pounding prevent the success of their journey.

She smelled a swampy cedar smell. Sometimes it was pleasant; other times it was revolting. Sarah heard wet, almost splashing noises, which sometimes resembled a sucking noise. It took tremendous power to move as swiftly as they were through the marsh. It seemed to Sarah it would have been impossible for her to travel alone. She related to that feeling she'd had as a child walking through mud and eventually falling over. Sarah had never known of this type of terrain in Minnesota. *Maybe they were not in Minnesota*, she thought, having no clue where they were.

June seemed to be keeping up. June had the personality of being as ready at the beginning of her ride or task as the end of it. Sarah wondered how far they would travel this first night, but she did not worry about June's endurance, because of her outstanding strength.

After what seemed to be an hour, the ground appeared to be less wet—not totally dry, but less wet. The most difficult part of ground had been covered, but now they were getting nearer to humans.

Suddenly, they stopped. The two male bigfoots drank out of a stomach-like vessel. Sarah turned to her pack, only now it was full of strawberries and mushrooms. The older bigfoot motioned for her to eat something from her pack by bringing his hand to his mouth and pretending to chew. He was so intense, she did what he indicated. Sarah offered them some food, which they took.

After the break, the older male picked up Sarah and placed her on the horse. June was still saddle-less but haltered with her reins. The only time Sarah rode bareback was during lessons when Jazabel was trying to strengthen Sarah's balance—and in the water a night ago. Jazabel had wanted Sarah to feel the horse move as June stepped higher or stretched out her stride. *Jazabel's training is proving to be helpful tonight. Hopefully, I'm ready for the challenge*, Sarah thought.

Sarah was enjoying the travel, although it was difficult. The moon lit up the trail, but Sarah's vision didn't allow her to see logs or puddles before June could. Sarah would have to trust June's footing. June would have to trust the bigfoots' footing. They traveled at a trot, sometimes quickly, which was not totally comfortable for Sarah. Very seldom would they slow down to a fast walk. Occasionally, they joined a graveled trail and moved with more ease.

Once, Sarah thought she heard the crackling of a fire, male voices, and laughter. But it was not the type of camp where the two bigfoots would consider leaving their companions. The waste and animal cruelty they had seen at these camps had at times caused them to chase the humans out by throwing rocks or growling.

The dominant male wanted to make sure the campers would not follow them. He stopped the caravan, crouched, and emulated a low, bass growl.

As he growled, Sarah started to feel shaky. The vibration seemed to set off her balance.

The elder male noticed the effects on Sarah. He yelped abruptly, and his son stopped immediately. In relief, Sarah's sensations stopped.

They started moving again. The dominant male watched with care over his father while letting the elder keep the pace. He did not want to overwork the older bigfoot.

In turn, with care, the older bigfoot watched over the horse and human. He did not want to overwork them.

The dominant male had already developed a plan. If they needed to speed up, he would journey on alone with the human and horse. But based on the male's observations so far, his father appeared to be in excellent shape.

Together, all four were covering the necessary ground.

CHAPTER 30

That night, Ben struggled with sleep. His thoughts raced.

He thought of his dogs. *Why didn't I bring the dogs? They could help me find Sarah,* he chided himself.

He thought about his son flying tomorrow—Mathew's first rescue mission, along with Levi's and Dylan's first observation flight. *Will they get sick, circling around and looking downward at the same time, as Sarah had on her first rescue flight?* He took mental note that he would need to remind them to eat before they took off.

Did Jazabel and I push Sarah too hard? No, he reassured himself. *Sarah said she felt ready for this.*

All those student fights Sarah has broken up over the years...what is she facing out there? Bugs are bad, and the evening air is beginning to get cooler. Is she in other danger? Did she break something? Ben hoped he would see her face early the next morning.

Over coffee, Ben briefed the boys. The coffee warmed his tired, concerned face. He reminded Mathew if he felt fatigued at all, he was to turn the airplane around and land.

Ben and Mathew already had a couple of long flight days behind them. Flying low created additional fatigue and potential danger. Emergency landings could be risky in the wooded area. Small, alternate airports had been mapped out and planned for landing if they could not land back at the original site.

Being safe in the air meant checking everything thoroughly while still on the ground. "Mathew, if you, Levi, or Dylan spot something, fly up to at least 500-feet elevation and keep circling until the search party can locate the area. While in the air, keep an eye open for trails or openings for the search party to get to Sarah." Ben had repeated the direction several times.

The crew engaged in one more check to ensure that everyone had working radios, headsets, and cell phones. Stara had it handled. She appeared to have been doing this all her life. Organizing a group of people and getting the equipment in the right hands was her natural strength. Her sleeping room had become the ground communication center.

CHAPTER 31

While they were traveling, the dominant male had the group stopped for what appeared to be a bathroom break. As Sarah watched, he partially tore up an asparagus fern, creating a hole. It looked as if the male was going to use the hole for a toilet.

He looked at her. Sarah diverted her eyes, but after the male relieved himself, she noticed he replaced the fern. Now she knew why bigfoots' waste was never found by humans. The males covered it, creating a natural compost. *Another way they take care of nature*, she thought.

They ate organically in what she has observed. It would appear the waste could be used directly as fertilizer.

On the farm, Ben and Sarah used horse compost for fertilizer, but they let it compost for a year before putting it on the garden. Apparently, the bigfoots' droppings did not burn the plants. *Maybe the hole was deep enough that by the time the root reached it, the manure was composted*, Sarah considered. *Seemed somewhat impossible without air or turning off the soil.* She felt it was clever, however it accomplished two objectives: it fertilized the plants and left behind no evidence of bigfoot.

Sarah had wondered how the bigfoot family had kept their dwelling clean from waste with seven individuals living within. She tried to clean out the horse shed as often as she could. Containing the mature helped keep down the fly population in the summer.

As she waited for her trailing companion, Sarah looked into the pine woods that consisted of a chaotic pattern of trees and colors. She observed larger trunks, then other different colors of brown and taupe bark. The subdued color was so peaceful and pleasing to view.

There was an occasional scatter of new young pine trees growing. This added a touch of green that connected with the ground and undergrowth. It was pastoral and serene, and Sarah imagined herself just one tiny splash in nature's artwork.

Moving within it, the vastness of the pine made it seem beyond her reach. The terrain had already changed several times. Aspen trees, with some tamarack pine, were scattered around the bog area, but now there were more pine trees.

She wished she could identify the trees and plants better. Missing that trail ride was not helping her learning curve, but she could live without knowing the plants' names. Knowing the clan of "Rainstorm" was invaluable.

Sarah did not know how long the bigfoots stayed in one place. The most likely answer was as long as they felt safe from intruders; but she had been an intruder, and they had brought her into their dwelling. Now she felt they were returning her for her own safety and their safety.

They had connected with her, and they felt a need to keep her safe, but they would have done that for any animal. Bigfoot felt the need to keep all creatures safe.

The human's safety meant to return her and the horse to her humans. Once the two bigfoots left her alone to find her humans, they only hoped she had the ability to survive—and the integrity not to tell. If she told, hopefully the bigfoot family would be reunited and out of the area before the curious humans could regroup and search for them.

Any acknowledgment of their species would unleash thousands of curious humans. The four of them, the horse, the human, and the two bigfoots were never meant to co-exist, but somehow, they felt a kinship to keep each other safe.

Soon they would part, but the bigfoot family left a mark on Sarah's heart. It was more than kindness. They had given her hope for humanity in their intimate connectedness— with their family and all of nature around them. Through their connections, they obtained the responsibility of the planet and its creatures' safety.

Safety from what? Sarah knew. Basically, from her kind: humans. They contained the very connectedness needed for the preservation of nature, which meant the human race. Their simplified being was far more complicated and magnificent than she had ever considered.

It was a two-way emotional road. They felt a kinship to her. With passing through her fear, they were able to witness her tenderness. They honored her existence.

As the group traveled together, the two males stopped and communicated. Sarah knew she heard the word for humans. After their discussion, they turned their direction. The older bigfoot gestured in the direction they were heading and nodded to Sarah. She could not doubt their decision making. She had no knowledge base from which to think differently. Sarah would simply trust them.

The older male had believed they could not get the humans close enough to other humans to successfully connect her with them without endangering themselves. The original plan felt uncomfortable. The bigfoots knew the last part of their travel would be dangerous, but they had heard an airplane in the distance sooner than they thought they would. They needed to rethink their actions for their own safety.

CHAPTER 32

Mathew had a quick conversation with his air crew. Dylan was in front as the scanner, and Levi was in back as the observer. It felt to them as if they were going deer hunting, receiving information on where they would post and walk. Helping each other reach their goal was natural for the brothers. But this time the goal was far more serious: finding their mother alive and well. Both missions could be deadly if not administered accurately.

Levi could change sides, considering the needs of the observation. Also, Levi and Dylan could change duties. The scanner needed to watch the trails and inform the pilot of any need to change coordinates. After checking in with Stara, the flight crew took off on schedule.

Jazabel and Henry left on horseback about the same time, along with Ben, Stara, Jerry, and a group of volunteers on foot.

Henry informed Jazabel that they would follow the group on foot until they saw a need to deviate from the trail.

To Jazabel, Henry seemed like many counselors at her equine program, although he was somewhat younger and cuter. They were "people persons" who loved horses.

Henry actually loved both plants and horses. He worked well with people, but they were his business, and sometimes they sucked his energy. He thought that Jazabel seemed different. She did not need all the attention that most needed. She was very independent and capable.

After close to an hour, Henry noticed a fork in the trail. One fork of the trail was more groomed. The other seemed to be an animal trail and was inviting to join.

Henry said to Jazabel, "I would like to take this trail just to see where it leads. Plus, let's allow the horses the freedom to find their footing and direction more than us reining them."

"Sounds good. I will follow your lead." Jazabel was far more distraught than she thought she would be. But she was so glad she could do something to search for Sarah and June, especially on horseback. It was a beautiful trail, she observed. She hoped Sarah had enjoyed it.

Jazabel confirmed the plan with Stara, and the horse team moved on. The horses stepped slowly over some branches and gently turned right to avoid a slightly open, brushy area.

Jazabel reflected on Sarah and June's training. *If Sarah remains confident, she could do this.* Jazabel reassured herself with these thoughts.

Occasionally, Henry would ask Jazabel a question such as, "How do you know Sarah?"

"She worked at the school I went to, plus I gave her riding lessons later on in life. Really, in a roundabout way, she is the reason I am a horse trainer." Jazabel offered no other information but asked Hank how he found his way to being a trail rider and plant expert.

The conversation lost momentum, and they rode on quietly.

After Henry and his horse, and Jazabel and Tank, milled around for most of the morning, Tank whinnied. Ahead on the trail was a saddle. Henry and Jazabel dismounted. Jazabel looked over the saddle and saw a fanny pack. "Should we open it or wait for Jerry?"

"I think we just open it. Any evidence would have been washed away. Plus, in opening it now, we may speed up the rescue." Jazabel opened the pack. She found a cell phone and Sarah's driver's license.

Fear filled her heart. She tried to contain it as she looked at Henry.

"What does this mean?" she tried to ask steadily.

"I don't know. But let's radio Stara and let her know what we found."

Jazabel radioed Stara, who informed Jerry, who asked for coordinates so that he could come out and look. Jazabel radioed back their location.

Jerry and Ben moved out as quickly as they could, as Stara returned to the command center. Plans for the search could be changing, and she needed to focus on the communication to all parties.

CHAPTER 33

At the same time the search party changed their plan, the bigfoot group would change their direction. They would head deeper into the forest towards an elderly couple with whom they had communicated for years. Communication may have meant leaving wild berries from the forest for a gratitude gift or picking up garden vegetables—communicating with each other without words, only with emotions.

This new plan would ensure the two male bigfoots could deliver the horse and human within the vision from the elderly couple's cabin. They knew the humans in the cabin were caring individuals. Their new human friend would be within human contact as soon as they left her at the location. The older bigfoot had always had his reservations about the female human traveling alone in the woods, but he thought this plan could work.

The elderly couple had lived deep in the woods for many seasons, and their home was surrounded by dense wood. Seldom were other humans traveling through the adjacent woods. The bigfoots and the human couple had coexisted as long as the humans had lived there. The couple had been placing fruit and vegetables in a wire mesh box with an easy opening latch for the bigfoots' convenience. This latch was designed for a creature with hands.

Over the years, the bigfoot family had double checked the area for traps, but never had there been one. And never had curious humans searched for them in the area. Their prints had never been cast, nor had their left-behind evidence of hair or fingerprints been analyzed.

The two bigfoots' new plan to travel to the cabin would mean more traveling, but the small caravan would be safer under the cover of the forest foliage. Again, they could zigzag across established human and animal trails. Plus, there was no sound of airplanes in that direction.

The horse appeared to be ready for the trip, and for most of the distance, the human could ride her. The energy of this horse matched the bigfoots' agility and capability. June was amazingly athletic. Her muscles seemed to develop even more over their short time in the forest. For her benefit, at least they did not have to travel through the cedar marsh again. They could use the human-made trails.

Sarah was confused by the direction change. She caught the elder bigfoot's eyes. He smiled back. Trying to reassure Sarah, he used words he believed Sarah understood. He started by using his language "caw, caw." Sarah knew it meant humans, then she heard him say a slow "human." Sarah smiled and nodded back, trusting her hairy tour guide to get her back home.

Sarah had no idea where she was besides on June's back. It felt good to be riding her. Sarah thought she had finally been in her own endurance race. Her running mates were two bigfoot males, but that was perfectly fine. They would cross the finish line together.

What images they were, the two males were slightly taller than she was even on June, a large Arabian.

June and I are heading home. The reality set in as she pondered this thought. Sarah would never forget her experience with this hairy family. She appreciated the many things they had taught her about herself and connectedness. She felt her confidence had grown, as she rode June in the early morning through the pine, aspen, and brush.

After many hours of the four traveling in the night, the sun broke through the wooded area, causing streaking lights through the pines. The smell of pine was remarkable. The humidity caused the pungent pine scent to linger longer in the air.

Sarah was surprised at her own endurance. They had been on the move since dark. They stopped for occasional replenishing periods—a moment of rest, food, and water. They would stop in areas that were similar in color to her endurance mates. As they leaned on a tree, their hair looked as if it was the moss growing on the tree.

Sarah questioned her own vision. *Bigfoots could hide anywhere*, she realized. It was obvious they knew their environment well and could conform themselves to it easily. Not that the bigfoot transformed magically into any new form. They created an illusion in which they were part of nature. Their hair became moss or a bush; their strength allowed them to move objects and hide under them.

How many times have I been close to a bigfoot while camping or hiking and never knew it? Sarah wondered, *When she was at lakes, were they near? Were they able to exist in the populated lake area?* Sarah had often looked into the pine area, as she had traveled by car through

Minnesota. She was looking for something moving, possibly a bear or moose.

This experience was totally different. She was part of the pine—part of the environment. It was simply enchanting to her. There was extreme quiet in the woods. June would occasionally crack a twig or rustle the underbrush. *Was it quiet because she was traveling with the bigfoots, and other animals were hiding?* She had never seen bigfoot eat meat, but she did not know. Their smell would have driven other carnivorous animals to their dwelling. *Was it because of respect? Did the creatures of the forest move out of the way out of reverence, thus opening the highway of forest for their speedy travel? Or maybe it was simply the early morning.* Sarah noticed when she was in the dwelling near a bigfoot, insects were not a problem. *Was it their pheromones? Or were insects simply afraid of them*? She began to wonder if all of nature, except humans, revered them and, out of respect, kept their distance.

Sarah eventually took off her mosquito netting top and placed it back in her backpack. It had hindered her vision.

June was magnificent as she traveled with these huge creatures. It was the consensus of the whole traveling party.

June had always been a little bored with her old pasture companion. Dundee was a noble and wise mate that June dearly loved and respected. Sarah treated her so well, but her life was repetitive. Jazabel had added some challenges in the training which helped with boredom. But this situation was better; the adventure was grand. And June loved every moment of it.

The pine trees were not as large as Sarah had thought. Many had lower branches slightly higher than the rider, but still she watched for the branches she had to duck. It seemed as if June was keeping her safe by avoiding a dangerously low branch or uneven ground. The bigfoot companions were dodging branches, but they could easily break branches as they ran alongside the horse team. The pine reached for the sky as the bigfoot males ran gracefully through the trees. It was obvious the three of them were caring for Sarah.

June was enjoying her athletic journey, sensing it was important. Sarah kept her attention on June and did not look around more than necessary, until two young deer came loping towards them on the path. The elderly bigfoot stopped the party. They stood motionless so as not to scare the deer or have the deer scare June. The two deer loped without sound for a few seconds. The silence was deafening, an abyss that encompassed the whole party.

Then within 20 feet, the young deer noticed the traveling caravan in front of them. They loped off the trail together. As all four watched, the deer quietly disappeared into the pine.

CHAPTER 34

Ben, Jerry, Jazabel, and Henry stood around the saddle. Jerry was the first to comment.

"This changes the search. Jazabel, can you tell me any reason why Sarah would take the saddle off June and leave her phone behind?"

"No, Sarah does not feel comfortable riding June bareback. I don't get it," Jazabel sadly replied.

Jerry turned to Ben. "This changes things. I cannot rule out an abduction. This is going to sound like a heartless question, but does June have some substantial value?"

Jazabel piped in. "Not really. Good papers, well trained, but no more than $4,000 in any market."

"Some people will do about anything for $4,000. Just to be safe, I'm going to send out officers to small cabins, farms, and livestock auction yards in the area with a photo of Sarah and June."

"Can you sell a horse without their papers?" Jerry asked.

Jazabel replied, "It might lower the amount, but horse people are trusting. If the previous owner says he will send them to you, people may buy a well-trained, good-looking horse."

"I don't see any signs of a struggle here, but the storm may have washed evidence away. Everything seems neatly stacked. Have you all checked any form of communication to see if someone is asking for a ransom?" Jerry asked.

"None of us have been home to check the mail," Ben replied.

"Can you get a trusted person to do that?" requested Jerry.

"Yes, I can have one of my workers check." With a heavy heart, Ben became more determined. He did not want to stop to eat or take water breaks.

Stara started attending to Ben's needs by instructing him that the volunteers needed to break. She used this as an excuse to give him breaks, too, when needed.

There was an unspoken fear in everyone's mind. *Were they going to find a body?* No one said it out loud. *Why was the saddle and phone left behind?* This was the question of the hour.

CHAPTER 35

The two bigfoots, human, and horse would soon reach their destination. The elder bigfoot was pleased that he could deliver both human and the horse safely but was a little sad that he would not have the human in their family anymore. He had enjoyed his time with her. He fashioned the human as a unique animal that had few skills to survive in the wilderness. He enjoyed looking into her pale-blue eyes and trying to read what emotions she had in any moment. She seemed like a kind human, and in his world, not much of a risk taker.

But in her world, she was attempting to take many risks—with many successes—today.

Sarah also was relieved, so happy to be seeing her family, but sadness crept in, knowing that she was leaving the bigfoot family. She acknowledged the somewhat brutal thought that she would never see them again, but she would never stop hoping for a reunion in her life. She'd had an experience that very few humans could have. She would love to share her story with her family but knew she was sworn to secrecy by her new friends, the bigfoot family, Raindrop. She would hope that she could use what information she had to help preserve their life and lifestyle.

But how can I do this without sharing my story? she wondered, knowing she could not and would not break their trust.

It was around noon when the four of them reached a ridge in the forest. There they stopped for a moment as a silence once again filled the forest and their hearts. The four walked into a small open area. There sat a metal basket with a latch, not locked but simply latched. Inside the basket were some kale, peppers, swiss chard, and a dozen or so apples, all in a cotton mesh sack.

That is where they got the cotton mesh bag, thought Sarah.

Down below the ridge was a small farmyard including a cozy looking log cabin with sheds on the side. A barn sat about 90 yards away from the house. Around the barn was a pine pole corral. The farmyard had a full sun garden. Everything about the farmyard looked as if it was planned for meeting basic needs.

Sitting at a picnic table on the ridge side of the farmhouse was a lady about 10 years older than Sarah. She looked up as the four reached the ridge. She did not look fearful. She sat quietly, almost content to see the strange group.

The dominant bigfoot uttered an affectionate and successful grunt. The elderly bigfoot slid Sarah off June. Sarah was gently supported by the elder bigfoot, as she had trouble finding a secure footing after riding all night. It amazed her how he predicted her needs. As he towered over her, he handed June's reins to Sarah. He bent over and touched his forehead to June's, then to Sarah's—holding the pose with Sarah for a long time. This bought Sarah to tears again; she was saying a final goodbye to her new friend. Sarah put her arms around her friend and gave him a hug. He encompassed her body with his arms and ever so lovingly hugged her back. She was excited to be going home but very moved by these creatures.

The dominant bigfoot did the same, touching his forehead to June's. Bending over even more to compensate for his massive size, he touched foreheads with Sarah without holding the pose for as long as the elder had. No hugs.

With the reins in Sarah's hand, he shooed Sarah with a gesture to move towards the lady. His need to see his bigfoot family tugged at him. The bigfoot males needed to move out quickly.

Sarah's eyes teared more as she looked back at the bigfoot, then forward to the lady. It was so bittersweet. She was so happy to see another human and so sad to say goodbye to her new friends. They had taught her so much. She thought again about connectedness, the caring for nature, the caring for strangers, the importance of all animals—her horses, a bird in the tree, a frog hopping across the road were all the same to them, simply precious.

She took a deep breath, gathering every ounce of courage she had left, and led June down the slightly sloped hill. June turned her head and gave what seemed to be a bass-level goodbye whinny to her new herd. Sarah walked slowly to the lady sitting at the picnic table.

As she walked forward, the lady stood up, purposely not to disturb anyone with a sudden movement. This was not her first time in seeing a bigfoot at her ridge, nor was it the first time she had ever seen a bigfoot send a human down to her.

Helen was a tall, thin, model-gorgeous woman, slightly older than Sarah. Helen momentarily thought about the first time she had seen the creatures. It was years ago when her young son had been lost in the woods for four days. Helen was sitting at the same table praying that she would see him again. The woman was angry at the woods for taking her son. She was also sad and scared. Then she looked up to see this elderly bigfoot holding her son's hand as they walked over the top of the ridge towards her. He reached down, picked up the boy, put his forehead on the boy's forehead, set him down, and shooed him towards his mother as one might shoo a hen back into the henhouse. The boy came running down the ridge, unscathed by his adventures in the forest.

The couple had felt an unbelievable amount of joy in the return of their amazing child. They informed the local authority their son had wandered back into the yard. Questions were asked, but eventually they were left alone with their joy.

To give thanks, Helen and her husband designed a makeshift food basket. She put a latch on it so animals without hands could not get the food, but the bigfoot family could open it. She began leaving her first picking of garden food and fruits for the bigfoots as a gratitude offering. If they were not interested in taking the food, she would give it to the creatures in the forest around the farm.

The day her son returned, the elderly bigfoot, many years younger, watched until the young boy was safely in his mother's arms. Today, the elderly bigfoot did the same thing, watching until Sarah and June were safely in Helen's presence.

Then, he clapped once.

To Sarah's surprise, Helen joined her in clapping twice in response.

The bigfoot clapped one final time, then disappeared into the woods.

CHAPTER 36

"Oh my, I know that smell. Why don't we call for my husband? He can put your horse in the corral while we go into the house. You can bathe, and we can call your family, dear."

For some strange reason, Sarah could only cry and nod her head yes.

Helen knew exactly who she was talking to. She had been listening to the news and heard a search party was looking for a lady and her horse that had gone missing on the trail ride about five days ago. Helen had hoped that she would not be called to give permission for the search party to come on their property. Although she wanted the lady found, she wanted the privacy of her forest to remain intact.

She had hoped if the search party started further southeast, maybe they would find the missing person before moving to her area. *Those bigfoots were good thinkers*, Helen reflected. *They made sure the lady was found safe, and their presence remained unknown.*

Now Helen needed the importance of their secrecy to be understood by this distraught person. Helen gave a quick holler to Edward, who was in the barn. He came out with the same expression that Helen had a few minutes ago.

"Will you please tend to the horse and make sure she is groomed well, while I take Sarah in and get her bathed, changed, and fed?" Helen asked. Sarah wondered how this woman knew her name, not thinking about the fact that it had been broadcast when she went missing.

"Yes, dear," he answered.

"Make sure you get all the leaves and loose hair from the horse. It has probably been awhile since it was groomed. The mare will enjoy it," directed Helen.

"Yes, dear," Edward replied. He followed her directions, taking the horse to the corral and giving it water and feed. Helen did not state why this was important in front of the female. But he knew the importance of removing any bigfoot evidence. They had discussed many times how blessed they were to have bigfoots in their woods. Helen and Edward would do nothing to change that.

After grooming June, he hung the halter on a hook in the barn. Helen was trying to communicate with Sarah, who at this point was extremely emotional. She told Sarah every action they were taking.

"We are going into the house now. My husband will take care of your horse."

Sarah cried and nodded her head "yes."

"After we are in the house, we will call your man. I saw him on the TV—a nice looking man. We will let him know you are safe and where you are."

Sarah continued crying and nodding her head "yes."

The two women walked inside the log farmhouse. It felt so warm and human.

"After we call, you can take a bath, and I will wash your clothes. Do you want me to call the authorities or your boyfriend?"

"I don't know. He doesn't always answer," Sarah whimpered.

Helen replied, "I think there was a number to call if anyone had information. I will try to find that number." Helen found the number and dialed the phone.

Stara picked up. "Hello, this is Stara."

"Hello, this is Helen Jackson. Sarah and her horse wandered onto our property. She is fine, just a bit emotional."

Stara asked to talk to Sarah. Sarah had a hard time saying anything except that she was okay and loved her.

Helen gave Stara directions to their farm. After Helen hung up, she started a bath for Sarah, laid out some fresh clothing, and washed Sarah's dirty clothing. With Sarah's permission, she would clean out the backpack, the clothes inside, and the pack.

While Sarah was bathing, Helen warmed up some soup. Sarah looked around the bathroom. It was nothing elaborate, but so comforting. She washed and conditioned her hair. She thought about washing in the lake. How refreshing that was, but the warm bathwater soothed her achy bones and calmed her. It had been a long night's ride. She slowly started to feel as if she could finally put sentences together.

After the bath, Sarah put on Helen's clothes. They were a bit long but did the job. Sarah walked into the kitchen and saw Helen at the stove.

"May I use your phone?"

"Of course."

Sarah called Ben, taking a deep breath and trying to sound coherent. "Hi Ben."

"Oh honey, are you okay?"

"Yes, I am fine. Just really tired."

Ben replied, "We are calling off the search party, and I should be there in a little over an hour."

"I will be so glad to see you. Can you bring the trailer?"

"I can, but that means not everyone can fit in the pickup. You will have to see the kids a little bit later."

"I talked to Stara already," Sarah clarified. "Please have them meet us at a convenient place, but not in public. I'm too distraught."

"Sure, anything you want. I have to go, but I'll be there in about an hour. I love you. I am so glad you are okay." Ben sounded tearful too.

After Sarah hung up the phone, Helen served her soup and sat down beside her at the table.

"You didn't seem surprised by my companions," Sarah commented.

Helen began with, "They are our co-habitants, our friends. May I tell you my story?"

Sarah found it nurturing to hear her speak. Of course she could tell Sarah her story. Helen began by explaining how they ended up making a home in the Minnesota woods. "We both come from affluent families. Edward still returns to Seattle. He sits on his family business board, a lumber company. When Edward's grandfather died, he gave the business to the other relatives. He gave Edward a voice on the board, a large amount of money, and this wooded area in Minnesota." She paused and then continued, "This gave Edward an opportunity to start his own mill or do whatever he wanted with the land." Helen believed Grandfather knew Edward's soul.

"The inherence sent us as a young couple to Minnesota to check out our newly-owned property. We wanted to see the layout of the land to make logistics plans for a new mill. Our first decision was to carve out a home as a farmstead rather deep in the property. We chose a spot that had a small nature clearing." With pride Helen reported, "Edward cleared out the driveway and used much of the wood from the cutting to build our home. It was deep in the woods. Edward thought when he started the mill, he would be close to home. But as we began to make a home in the woods, we began to feel it was not only ours. You may know what I mean, it belongs to the creatures and the beauty of nature itself."

It was an easy decision. With the money Edward made from his position on the board and what money Helen had from her family, they could live simply in their new home. Which they did. Eventually, Helen gave birth to a boy.

"I believe at this time in life, we had our first encounter with a bigfoot." Helen continued telling her story. "It was a very muddy spring when I went into labor. Edward and I were in the car heading down to the hospital," Helen stated. "To our dismay, we got stuck in a low spot. Edward wanted to get out and push while I drove. I was so afraid, I pleaded for him to stay in the car with me. As he was rocking the car back and forth by putting it into drive then reverse, trying to move the car out of the mud, we felt a thump in the back of the car, and it surged us forward. Relieved, we plowed out of the mud and rushed to the hospital. We never looked back to see what caused the propelling thump. After our son was born, Edward went to the car to get my bag and saw two huge marks on the car. Crazy as it seems, we now believe we were pushed out of the mud, possibly by a bigfoot. It truly was the beginning of our lifetime impacted by their existence."

Helen explained that they really did not think about it much after returning home from the hospital. The small family continued to make their farmstead a home for the three of them. "Our little guy loved exploring around the farmyard. He had been given parameters in which to play, and he generally followed them. In the summer before kindergarten, Jared was playing outside. He saw a young bunny and was mesmerized in the chase. He disappeared into the woods."

Helen's voice weakened as she explained how the couple searched for him. The local community had participated in the search, but there was no evidence of her child to be found. On the fourth day he was missing, Helen was sitting at the small picnic table. She hated the wilderness and blamed it for taking her son. She was sad and angry. She had been feeling she was totally alone in this world, but at that moment, she felt not totally alone in her surroundings. Helen happened to look up at the tree line and saw a bigfoot bringing her son home. Of course, the bigfoot was much younger than the elder bigfoot was now.

Helen had often thought about this scene. The adult held her son's hand in his right hand and a bigfoot child's hand in his left. Was the elder bigfoot who brought Sarah back the adult or the child? She did not know how fast they aged.

Over the years, the couple recognized the elder bigfoot. They even clicked responses of gratitude to each other. "It seemed that it was easy to emotionally communicate with them without words," she shared. When seeing her child, Helen yelled for Edward. She did not care if she would be harmed; she ran to her boy.

That wonderful day, the dark creatures disappeared into the wood, not waiting for a thank you. Her son was returned unharmed—very stinky, but unharmed. The smell was unforgettable, much like a very strong, old pot smell, skunky in a way.

Jerad, their boy, began sharing stories of his adventure. He reported bigfoot saved him from being attacked by a bear. Jared would mimic the loud roars the bigfoot father made. He was glad the bigfoot was on his side, although the bear was not hurt, just scared away. He talked about sleeping in a woven wooden dome. He wanted Edward to make a dome, but they could never bend big enough boughs. Edward tried soaking the branches in water, but he still could not get them right.

Jared would click his tongue against the roof of his month on rare occasions, and sometimes there would be a click back from the woods, which would delight Jared. Limited in his young language development, he would try to talk about bigfoot communication. Or sometimes he would simply show by example, and he would bang big branches together and laugh.

Helen and Edward called their boy "little bigfoot." When hearing that he would clap once at them, through trial and error, they learned to clap back twice, then Jared would clap once again. While Helen would be in the garden, Jared would clap. The ritual made both parties feel closer.

Jared was a unique boy. He enjoyed himself outdoors but also enjoyed his visits with his relatives in the city. The summer he was 10, he asked to stay longer in Seattle. His uncle would drive him back before Labor Day weekend. On the trip back, they both died in a car accident. After that accident, Helen sat at the picnic table blaming the city for her son's death.

Sometimes crying, sometimes just sitting, but she knew her sadness filled the air. When she sat at her picnic table, she again felt she was not totally alone in her environment. It really did not matter to her, she mourned for her "little bigfoot."

Edward tried to make her feel better, but he was not having an easy time either. His brother and son had died. Little bigfoot—Jared—was their life.

They would regularly put food in the basket. Jared had loved feeding his bigfoot friends. Helen was so thankful for the extra five years they had given her with her boy.

Edward continued trying to bend wood into a shelter, but mostly he carved forest creatures, including trolls and bigfoots out of the fallen trees. Helen pointed to a carving in the kitchen to demonstrate the work.

As Sarah looked around, she saw Helen's story unfold in hand carved figurines. Helen noticed Sarah's awareness and said, "I think it was Edward's way of preserving Jared and dealing with the grief."

Helen stopped telling her story and looked at Sarah. "May I show you something?"

"Of course," responded Sarah. She was feeling more relaxed as she listened to the story.

Helen got up and walked into her bedroom, coming back with a twig, woven, ornament-type object. The object contained dried flowers. "I found this in my bigfoot food container. With the latch closed. The flowers are lilac and daisies. I researched the flowers, and they are known to have healing power. How did bigfoot know I needed healing, and how did they know about the flowers?"

Sarah had finished her soup. "I know; the female used tannin on my wound. I wondered the same thing," Sarah quietly stated.

"I believe we have all known the value of plants and nature, but in our current lives, we think things have to be research-based before they truly work," Helen suggested.

Sarah responded to something that was stated earlier, "I stayed in the tree-woven shelter. I do not know if it was the same one your son stayed in. It was miles away."

"I hope it was the same one. That would make me happy. When I was cleaning your backpack and washing your clothes, I found something in the backpack. I put it back."

Sarah got up, got her pack, and bought it back. Amongst the freshly clean clothing was an amulet. It was made of cedar, and inside the cedar casing was what seemed like a dried star flower and dried wild mint. "It's wonderful. What do you think it is?"

Helen replied, "I think they made it for you. Cedar is

strong, mint helps with trauma. The star flower is a simple flower that brings joy to the north. I think a bigfoot is telling you to be strong and that you bring joy to others."

"It is truly lovely, and it smells so good. I will cherish it. I wonder who made it? The elderly bigfoot took me under his care."

"They all saw your value. It may have been a family process." The statement made by Helen brought tears to Sarah's eyes.

"Please feel free to tell me about your experience with the bigfoots. You must be careful to tell no one else," Helen pleaded.

"I know, I promised them I would keep their secret. They were so kind to me. I didn't realize it at first, because I was so afraid. But they did nothing to harm me. In fact, they took care of me."

"You promised them? What does that mean, Sarah?"

Sarah explained how the oldest bigfoot communicated with her and tried to teach her their way of communication. She had promised him she would not tell other humans of their existence. Sarah then made the same gesture, containing the sounds and sealing her mouth closed.

"That is very interesting, I knew somehow they communicated with my son." Then Helen continued with her original thought, "Your family will be coming soon to get you, what do you intend to tell them?"

Sarah confessed she was confused and had no idea what to say.

"When little Jared was brought back to us by a bigfoot, we encouraged him to tell us everything, but we told him we needed to protect the bigfoot family since other people would simply not understand. We wanted to protect our son. We didn't know how society would take his story. We knew search parties would be sent out to look for the bigfoot group, which would be an inconvenience, but more importantly they would analyze and try to interrogate Jared ruthlessly. We needed to protect him. So, we told him to tell the law enforcement he wandered into the forest until he found his way back home. Which was kind of the truth," Helen paused. "Could you tell your family, you cannot remember much, but wandered the forest until you found us?"

"I think after my head injury, the confusion could be used as a symptom of my concussion. My family would probably believe that. You know what children generally think about their parents. I could give June credit for finding our way here. I just have so much to share and to understand."

"Share it by doing it, Sarah. Plus, you can come back and talk to Edward and me anytime. Would that work for you?"

"Do you think I could call? I seem to need to process things on the spot."

"Yes, please do, anytime. Can we agree on the bigfoot secrecy?"

"Yes, I have already given my word to the elder bigfoot. May I see June? She was fabulous through all of this."

"Of course, you may." Helen took Sarah out to the barn.

CHAPTER 37

Once again, Sarah was tearing up as she talked to her very clean and well-fed June. She told her what a good girl she was—and a perfect endurance horse. Sarah was sure not every horse could keep up with a bigfoot.

Ben's pickup and the horse trailer pulled into the driveway. Following the trailer was a police car, and following that was a car full of Sarah's children. They had been determined to see her.

Helen leaned over to Sarah and said, "Remember: confused, forgetful, and wandering."

"Don't worry. I am too emotional to say much of anything," Sarah said tearfully.

It was a tearful reunion with many hugs. Stara asked her mother if she had any injuries.

Sarah replied, "I think I bumped my head on the first day of the trail ride."

Stara turned to her mother's head and said, "It appears to be healing, but you should have that looked at. Levi and Dylan told us how dense the forest looked from above when they were flying further south. They couldn't imagine you being in it with June."

Dylan commented, "It is amazing Mom found her way to the Jackson's."

"I have to give June much of the credit. She found the trails to follow and protection from the storm for us."

"Lead mare, that is June. She looks so clean," replied Levi.

"I had Edward feed, water, and groom June," interjected Helen. "For her travels, she wasn't worse for wear."

"What do you know about her travels?" Jerry piped up as he joined the group.

"I was just assuming that they must have traveled a distance from here to the trail ride, nothing otherwise," added Helen.

After a moment, Jerry introduced himself. "I am really glad you're safe. I will need to take a statement from you after you are feeling better."

"I really don't have a lot of details," Sarah responded.

"After being gone so long, maybe you should have your wound looked at by the hospital staff. Just to make sure it is not affecting memory." It felt like déjà vu for Jerry. He had been in this yard many years ago with a young boy who only knew that he had wandered the forest for many days.

"Right now, I just want to go home, put June in the pasture, and spend time with my family," Sarah told him.

"That's fine," Jerry replied. "No crime was committed. I just need a statement. It still wouldn't hurt to have your head looked at. I see a slight black and blue mark on your forehead also."

Sarah put her hand up and touched it, as she remembered watching the little bigfoot mimic her. A slight smile came over her face.

"I just have one quick question," Jerry added. "Why did you take the saddle off of June and leave your phone with it?"

"Is the saddle okay?" she asked Ben. "It was a birthday gift," she informed Jerry.

"Yes, it just needs a little cleaning. Don't even worry about it," answered Ben.

Sarah turned to Jerry and said, "I do not remember anything about the fall or saddle. Maybe I left it to let someone know I had been there."

Levi piped in, "I am really impressed you rode bareback all this way through the woods."

"So am I, and I am so proud of June. She took care of me."

Sarah thanked Helen and Edward for everything. Helen gave Sarah her number. On the paper, Helen wrote, "Call, I can help you with the statement."

Before loading June onto the trailer, Sarah rubbed her Arabian's face and touched her forehead to June's. June whinnied back in response.

As Ben and Sarah headed back to the farm, Ben looked over at Sarah who sat quietly in the pickup. Her children were following in another vehicle. Sarah felt miles away from them, wishing she could be surrounded by them.

"How are you? You are so quiet, Sarah," Ben inquired.

She was staring into the forest and said, "I am so happy to be with you. I am trying to put my story together."

Ben commented, "You are just tired, dear."

"Yes, let's stop for coffee so I can connect with the kids before they all scatter."

Sarah thought: *Nothing is more magnificent than their simplicity and connectedness. They gave me back my humanity.*

As she gazed into the woodland, she wondered: *are they safe, together, and connecting?*

EPILOGUE

Stara and Sarah were sitting on the huge deck of the cabin, which had become a peaceful solitude throughout the pandemic and now in the aftermath.

Stara, her brothers, Ben, and Jazabel had noticed a difference in Sarah after her disappearance. Her relationship with June was phenomenal, and her confidence in her riding was unlike in any other period in her life. She consistently touched base with her family.

But whether riding or just sitting on the deck, Sarah would enter a silence of searching. She would bring her companions with her by a touch or hum. When returning from the silence, there was an unmatchable smile on her face.

If June could only talk, maybe she could share what was being searched for all those countless times while she gazed into the evening's vastness.

Tonight, as Stara and Sarah sat in silence, a clap came out of the wooded area—just to the right of the cabin. Sarah sat up more directly and clapped back twice. Another clap returned from the wooded area. Sarah got up and started walking towards the darkness of the woods.

"What are you doing?" asked Stara.

"Just stay here," answered Sarah.

"Mom..." Stara started to argue.

"Just stay here," Sarah responded firmly yet kindly.

Sarah clapped once, and two claps returned from the darkness. She scurried after the sound while clapping back once.

Stara peered over the railing, trying to understand what her mother was doing. She thought she could see the back of her mother's jacket at the trees' edge, where she seemed to have stopped.

Eventually, Sarah yelled up to Stara, "Come here, but try not to be afraid."

What the hell is going on? Has Mother lost it? Stara slowly walked to her mother, who was communicating to something seemingly invisible by talking a little and using her hands a whole lot.

While walking towards her mother, Stara gradually made out a large figure standing a few feet deeper in the woods, directly in front of Sarah.

Sarah turned around to Stara. She took her by the shoulder and said, "This my friend, Raindrop." Sarah made a gesture with her hand, then clucked her tongue, making the sound of a drop hitting a puddle. "He protected me when I fell from June."

Stara's mouth dropped open as she viewed this elderly, 8-foot tall creature who was seemingly smiling at her mother, then her. He twisted his mouth and tried saying, "Hello, human."

Sarah laughed and touched him. Stara tried grabbing Sarah to move her away from the beast, but Sarah dodged the grab. Sarah gestured as if holding a baby, touched herself, and pointed to Stara, saying, "Stara."

The creature tried to say Stara, but the "r" seemed to be difficult.

"Say, 'Hi,' Stara. I will tell you the story later. And breathe," instructed Sarah.

Stara stood dumbfounded and said, "Hi." She watched this huge creature touch foreheads with her mother for more than a moment, then gently embrace her. The embrace was interrupted by a loud, deep hoot coming from a distance. The creature returned the hoot. The sound vibrated through Stara.

The creature turned to her mother, bent down, and touched his forehead to hers one last time, saying, "Sarah." He quietly turned around and gracefully walked into the dark wooded area.

Stara looked questioningly at her mother. "Bigfoot?"

As tears rolled down her cheek, Sarah responded, "I think my old friend came to say his last goodbye."

Sarah folded her arms around Stara, and they walked backed to the deck. While they walked, her mother returned her last two claps to her bigfoot friend, Raindrop.

BIO

Linda Stutrud Scheet was born in Rugby, North Dakota, and lived on her family farm until at the age of 17, when she enrolled at Minneapolis College of Art and Design.

After both rural and urban experiences in her early adulthood—and traveling around United States and Mexico—Linda returned to her rural roots. With her growing family of a husband and three children, she lived on a farm for 15 years, until circumstances led her to uproot her life.

Linda decided to advance her education at Minnesota State University, Moorhead. During and after receiving her master's degree in social work, she worked as a school social worker—helping at-risk students and their families. While in the educational system for 20 plus years, Linda's life was enriched by residing in an old farm-style house near the Red River in Fargo, North Dakota.

After retirement, Linda moved to a rural setting in Cass County, North Dakota. She is living with her belief in connectedness—of family, friends, animals, and nature. With her significant other, they are raising three horses, one dog, and thirteen chickens.

Made in the USA
Coppell, TX
20 November 2020